Santa Daddy

Also by Keira Andrews

Contemporary

The Spy and the Mobster's Son
Honeymoon for One
Beyond the Sea
Ends of the Earth
Arctic Fire

Lifeguards of Barking Beach
Flash Rip
Free Wind

Holiday
The Christmas Deal
The Christmas Leap
The Christmas Veto
A Baby for Christmas
Only One Bed
Merry Cherry Christmas
Santa Daddy
In Case of Emergency
Eight Nights in December
If Only in My Dreams
Where the Lovelight Gleams
Gay Romance Holiday Collection

Sports
Kiss and Cry
Reading the Signs
Cold War
The Next Competitor
Love Match
Synchronicity (free read!)

Gay Amish Romance Series
A Forbidden Rumspringa
A Clean Break
A Way Home
A Very English Christmas

Valor Duology
Valor on the Move
Test of Valor
Complete Valor Duology

Historical

Kidnapped by the Pirate
Semper Fi
The Station
Voyageurs (free read!)

Paranormal

Kick at the Darkness Trilogy
Kick at the Darkness
Fight the Tide
Defy the Future

Fantasy

Barbarian Duet
Wed to the Barbarian
The Barbarian's Vow

SANTA DADDY

KEIRA ANDREWS

Santa Daddy
Written and published by Keira Andrews
Cover by Dar Albert
Formatting by BB eBooks

ISBN: 978-1-988260-74-7

Acknowledgments and Dedication

Thanks to Anara, Mary, DJ Jamison, and Leta Blake. This one's for everyone who loves the holidays as much as I do. Fa la la la la! <3

Chapter One

MALL SANTAS WEREN'T supposed to be hot.

Heart thudding from his run through town, Hunter stopped short inside the storage room, the back door to the parking lot slamming shut behind him with a gust of frigid air. He blinked at the vision standing in front of him like a mirage amid the stacks of dusty boxes and crates.

Was he still asleep? Was this a fever dream? Because mall Santas were supposed to be old and kind of short and schlubby. It was the law of the universe or something.

Yet this Santa—probably mid-forties and wearing shiny black boots, red velvet pants with fuzzy white cuffs, and a matching red velvet coat hanging open—was something out of a *Details* lumberjack photo shoot or one of those fireman calendars Hunter's mom got every year that he used to secretly jerk off to as a teenager.

A white tank top stretched over Santa's broad, muscular chest, dark hair peeking out the top of the cotton, his nipples hard and skin a warm olive. His short hair and full, trimmed beard were way more pepper than salt, but the scattered silver highlights were crazy sexy. He had to be at least six-two and towered over Hunter, arching a dark eyebrow.

Please ask if I've been naughty or nice.

"About time."

Hunter blinked at him, his porno fantasy evaporating as he tried to catch his breath. "Huh?"

"You're late," Santa accused gruffly.

"Oh. Right." A burst of anxiety froze out the sizzle of lust that had warmed Hunter's veins. "I know, sorry." He panted softly, pulling off his wool hat. His hair fell over his forehead, and he pushed a strand out of his eye. "I overslept."

Santa stared at him as if he was profoundly stupid and/or pathetic. "It's almost noon."

What are you, my father? Hunter squirmed with embarrassment. He despised being late, but he couldn't turn back time now and erase the last twenty minutes. He hadn't *intended* to stay up until almost four playing *God of War,* and then he'd set his alarm for ten p.m. instead of a.m. because he was a tool.

He knew this—he didn't need inappropriately hot Santa to remind him. Mall Santas were also supposed to be jolly and kind, not judgy assholes. He rolled his eyes. "Whatever. You're not my boss. And where's Mr. Tremblay?"

"Broke his hip."

"Oh. Shit, that sucks." Old Mr. Tremblay had been Pinevale's mall Santa for as long as Hunter could remember. "Um, I'm Hunter. Hunter Adams." A couple hours north of Toronto, Pinevale wasn't so small that he knew everyone in town, but Hunter definitely would have remembered seeing this guy around. Where on earth had John found him?

"I'm Mr. Spini."

A first name was apparently unforthcoming. Who did this guy think he was? Hunter was twenty-three, not some kid. Before Hunter could say as much, John Singh bustled in through the mall entrance beyond the boxes, pushing wire-rimmed glasses up his nose and wearing an incredibly ugly reindeer sweater with fuzzy antlers. In his fifties, he and his husband, Desmond, lived a few blocks from Hunter's mom. He was short, stout, and always in a hurry, but was usually smiling. Not now, though.

"Hunter! Finally."

"I know, I know. Sorry." Hunter's face went hot as he shrugged off his backpack and pulled out the ridiculous candy-cane tights. Keeping his head down, he unlaced his boots and stripped off his jeans, goosebumps spreading over his skin in the chill of the storage room, the floor freezing. As he tugged the tights over his boxer briefs, he looked up and met Santa's gaze, which swept down Hunter's body.

"What?" Hunter shoved his socked feet into the too-tight black slippers with toes curved inward and golden bell on the ends. He muttered, "I look lame, I know."

Not all of us can look unfairly hot in these costumes.

Santa said nothing as John handed him the padded belly, long white beard, and red velvet hat with white trim. "Final touches."

Hunter buttoned the green velvet jacket that barely covered his ass and junk, the fluffy white cuffs landing two inches above his wrists. The seams were snug around his shoulders, and he couldn't really lift his arms. Last time he played elf was his senior year of high school, and he hadn't realized how much he'd grown in five years. He'd been a late bloomer, although usually he still felt like that pimply, bony kid.

"Good thing this is the last year for Santa's Village." Not that he'd be desperate enough to be an elf again next year. He was getting a real job in January if it killed him. A job that didn't require a humiliating costume.

Then he felt like a dick and quickly added, "I just mean because the costume's too small on me now. It sucks that the mall's closing." Even though it was the Mall That Time Forgot and was super depressing.

John had been the mall manager for ages, and he'd been a good boss. When Hunter had emailed him on the off chance he had seasonal work, he hadn't been thinking of playing elf again, but beggars couldn't be choosers and all that. He'd been lucky John had given him the job at all.

John waved his hand. "No offense taken. Gotta move with the times. Did you hear they're putting in a Marshall's and an Outback Steakhouse? And the old grocery store on Lake Street is shutting down and a big one's going here. It'll be box stores: Treeview Plaza instead of Treeview Mall. The new owners are keeping me on to manage, so I'm good. Security, snow removal—there's still a lot to coordinate." Sweat beaded on his brown skin, and he swiped a hand over his forehead. "It's a sauna out there—the heater's stuck on high."

Hunter shivered. "Yet it's freezing back here."

John grimaced. "Same in my office and the bathrooms, but obviously there's no sense in paying to fix it. The last day is December thirty-first, and then they're tearing this old dog down and rebuilding come spring. But first we need to give this mall one last Christmas to remember. Right, team?"

Santa buckled the wide black belt around his fake belly, his long white beard obscuring the lower part of his face. He muttered, "Why did I agree to this?"

"Because you're a good friend who's doing me a favor at the last minute. I'll find someone else for next weekend, I promise. Plus all the money's going to buy toys for kids and turkey dinners. With the factory closing down this summer, it'll be a lean Christmas for a lot of folks. So that's why you agreed to this, for the record."

Santa only grumbled under his breath in response, jamming the hat on his head.

"Wait. *All* the money?" Hunter's stomach dropped. "Are we not getting paid?" After three unpaid internships in Toronto since he'd graduated university and still no actual jobs, he'd come home early to Pinevale for the holidays to live in his old bedroom and play mall elf one more time. At least he'd be getting minimum wage—or so he'd assumed.

"No, no!" John clapped Hunter on the shoulder. "You'll be paid. But Mr. Tremblay had offered to give up his salary this year and donate it to Toys and Turkeys—that's what we're calling the fund. Nick followed suit."

"Oh." Hunter glanced at Santa—this Nick Spini, who watched him with a disdainful sneer.

Shit. Was Hunter being selfish? Doing eight-hour shifts Saturday and Sunday for two weekends would give him money for presents for his mom, sister, and his new niece. He'd been hoping to find some other seasonal work during the week since Pinevale wasn't big enough to warrant a full-time Santa's Village, and with the tiny, ancient mall closing, there wasn't enough demand for pictures with Santa for more than the two weekends.

Granted, he'd spent the majority of the last four days since he'd taken the Greyhound home playing video games and eating Doritos instead of job hunting, but he'd just wanted to not think about the mess of his life for a little while. The internship he'd just quit had expected twelve-hour days just like the other places, and he was burned-out.

Familiar acid flooded his belly. Before Hunter could explain that he needed to make money for working after more than a year of interning for "experience" and "connections" and to "get his foot in the door"—only to have said doors slammed in his face as soon as he tried to actually earn a living, Nick said, "Can we get this over with?"

Instead of calling him out for being a bag of dicks, John only laughed. "That's the holiday spirit. Come on, Grinch. Time to grow that heart. I know you're not used to being around people, but just think, What would Eric have said and done? Then do that."

Nick huffed, and Hunter couldn't tell if he was pissed or kind of laughing? Wondering who Eric was, Hunter grabbed his elf hat and followed Nick out of the storeroom after they stashed their stuff in an old staff locker. His eyes were drawn to how the red velvet stretched across Nick's wide shoulders. He was a mountain of a man.

They made their way over the ugly brown brick floor, a weird cobblestone that was probably done in the seventies before there were accessibility laws. Half the stores had closed already, and although John had hung wreathes and garlands on the brown brick walls, Treeview Mall was clearly in its death throes.

It was windowless, low-ceilinged, and one story in a square horseshoe shape, like a time capsule of ugly seventies design. The handful of old men who spent hours a day in the tiny food court area with only two greasy food options—Roy's Burgers or Donut Time—watched silently as they passed, paper coffee cups in front of them. The peppy strains of "All I Want for Christmas is You" played through the mall's speakers, Mariah's voice echoing on the cobblestones.

The women who worked in La Belle Style, the old-lady clothing store that was sticking it out to the mall's bitter end, gathered in the doorway as they passed. "Hunter!" Mrs. Buckingham called. "Don't you look adorable!"

He gave his mom's friend a weak smile, cringing as he felt hundreds of eyes on him as they reached the line of families, restless kids exclaiming in excitement at seeing Santa. The kids squealed and cried, "Santa!" and Nick jolted before waving at them as if remembering *he* was Santa.

Tugging down his green jacket, Hunter felt like a bigger loser than usual as he followed in Nick's wake. Hunter was five-eight, so not *super* short or anything, but he was a scrawny kid in comparison. He was blond and could barely grow a beard, and Nick was teeming with hair and muscles and manliness. Which was weird for Santa Claus, but he was working it, definitely catching the attention of the moms waiting in line in front of Santa's Village.

Hunter supposed elves weren't supposed to be manly, but the merry *ding!* of the golden bells on his shoes with each pinched step didn't do anything for his self-esteem. Not that he was planning on picking up guys at the mall—he was hopeless in that department. Still, he felt as gangly as he had back in high school.

The village was an ancient gingerbread house sort of thing that had seen far better days, but John had strung it with tons of colored Christmas lights and garlands to cover how faded and decrepit the painted plywood was.

Nick settled himself on a wide bench. The line of people were roped off at the end of the fake candy path that wound through little snow-sprayed Christmas trees, so at least in the village there was a bit of breathing room. Hunter was surprised there was such a sizable crowd, but there wasn't much to do in Pinevale.

He frowned at the bench. "No throne thingy?"

John shook his head. "The whole sitting-on-Santa's-lap thing is inappropriate these days." He pointed to the bench, which had a backrest. "This way the kid can sit beside Santa, and there's room on both sides if siblings want to come up together."

"No one's sitting on my lap," Nick growled.

Hunter rolled his eyes. "You realize you have to be nice to the kids, right?"

Nick only stared at him above his fake white beard. His eyes were a steely gray flecked with yellow, and it was *really* annoying how hot he still was even though he was apparently a dick.

John clapped his hands, putting on a big grin. "Okay, showtime!" As he led Hunter back down the path, he whispered, "Nick's a grump, but his bark is worse than his bite."

Hunter wanted to ask how John knew him, but there wasn't time. "If you say so."

"Trust me. Okay, you remember how it goes? I take the money from the parents, and you ask the kids their names and escort them to Santa." He peered around. "Where's our photographer… There she is."

"Hey, guys!" Courtney Campbell joined them with a smile, her dark ponytail swishing and a big camera around her neck. She was in her forties and ran Pinevale's little photography store. She wore jeans and a snowman sweater, and it didn't seem fair that she didn't have to dress up. "Hunter, didn't expect to see you pulling on the candy-cane tights again."

Well, I'm almost twenty-three, I can't get a real job, I'm freeloading off my sister in TO, I have a shit-ton of student debt, I honestly hate working in an office, I'm still a virgin, and I have no clue what I want to do with my life, so why not make the humiliation complete by being a mall elf again?

He managed to smile. "Yeah. Me either."

"Hunter's doing me a favor," John said. "I had to beg, but he agreed."

Hunter gave him a grateful smile for the lie. "It's no problem."

John winked at him and turned to the line of people. "Sorry for the delay, folks! Rudolph got a flat!" The crowd laughed agreeably, and John murmured to Hunter, "Fa la la la la!"

Gah la la la la was more like it, but Hunter slapped on a smile, trying to choke down the worry about money and his future and what he'd do after the holidays. His mom would let him stay as long as he wanted, but what was he going to *do*? What did he even *want* to do?

He'd gotten an English lit degree because that's what he was good at, and it was useless in the real world aside from ticking off the requirement of most companies to have a BA in *something*. He couldn't even get an entry-level job, and he'd worked his ass off at those internships.

His gut twisted, pulse kicking up and his breath catching. Fuck, he just felt so out of control.

"It's Santa!" a little girl squealed, jerking Hunter back to the present. His life was an aimless shit-show, but at least he had *a* job to do. He took a deep breath and pulled on his green elf hat, the white fuzzy brim already too hot on his forehead. No matter. Even with a grumpy, brawny, stupidly sexy Santa to put up with, he was going to be his best elf self. With bells on—literally.

Chapter Two

SITTING ON THE too-hard bench, Nick watched as Hunter reached to straighten his elf hat. His green jacket rode up, giving Nick an excellent view of his perky, rather spectacular ass. He was quite pretty, what with his golden hair wisping over his forehead, a round face and pink lips, freckles on his nose, and deep blue eyes. Too bad he was apparently one of those spoiled millennials who showed up late and only cared about money.

Hunter looked to be in his twenties and probably still lived at home. By his mid-twenties, Nick had been working full time for years and owned a truck and a house. It hadn't been easy, and he'd worked his way up, learning about forestry and eventually tree farming. He hadn't expected anything on a silver platter. People of all ages these days seemed more entitled than ever, and Nick had no patience for any of it.

Well, Hunter wasn't Nick's business, or his problem. He was playing Santa for two days, and two days only. When the usual Santa had fallen that morning, John had called in a panic, and considering John and Desmond were Nick's only friends, he'd given in. So this weekend he'd have to deal with people whether he liked it or not.

He thought of John's instructions: What would Eric have said and done?

As Nick watched Hunter lead a little red-headed girl along the path toward him, he had to smile to himself, hearing Eric's voice—low, with a mischievous hint to his Scottish brogue.

I'd say you're being a miserable grouch and that you need to remove the stick from your ass, stat. That's my professional medical opinion.

Of course Eric was gone, so what did he know? But no, he was right, and Nick made an effort to smile genuinely at the girl, who clung to Hunter's hand. Maybe Nick's smiling skills were rusty, since Hunter said to her, "It's okay, Jessica. Santa's really friendly, I promise." He shot Nick a pointed look, eyebrows raised as if daring Nick to prove him wrong. Okay, perhaps there was a bit of sass there, not just eye-rolling millennial petulance.

Nick cleared his throat, pitching his voice a little higher and softer than usual, mimicking the way Eric had spoken to young children. "Hi there, Jessica. It's wonderful to meet you. Do you want to sit down and tell me what you'd like for Christmas?"

As Jessica hesitantly told him about wanting a sled and some kind of doll that was probably the latest fad, Nick nodded and smiled and pretended he knew exactly what she was talking about. From the corner of his eye, he was aware of Hunter watching, and when Nick glanced at him while he and Jessica shifted for their picture, Hunter's cheeks went red, and he hurried back down the candy path.

The picture was taken as Hunter brought up the next kid, and Nick smiled and nodded to the steady stream of children coming to sit with him. He also tried to ignore Eric in his head.

Admit it—the kids are adorable. You don't hate this. Especially with the sexy elf eye candy.

Eric had always called him on his shit, and eight years after his death, his voice in Nick's head was a familiar comfort. It wasn't *real,* of course, and it wasn't always there. But Eric would show up once in a while, usually when Nick needed a swift kick in the ass.

Yes, sometimes Daddy needs the spanking.

He snorted out loud, and Hunter, who had brought up another girl, glared and hissed, "What are you laughing at?" His fair cheeks flushed red, and when he had the girl seated, he tugged at the hem of his green jacket. Clearly, he was uncomfortable in the too-small costume, but he also seemed anxious and jittery in his own skin. Any traces of sass vanished, replaced by a flash of raw vulnerability.

Nick instinctively wanted to reassure him, but before he could, the little girl was providing detailed evidence of her being very, *very* good and deserving of soccer cleats and a princess dress with puffy sleeves she really, *really* wanted so, *so* much.

The stream of kids seemed unending, and Nick's ass was numb and his entire body uncomfortably damp with sweat by the time John closed off the line and put up a sign saying they'd be back in half an hour. Nick's cheeks actually hurt from all the smiling, and he couldn't wait to take off the beard and hat.

While John grabbed them lunch, Nick and Hunter retreated to the storeroom. As soon as they were inside, Hunter rounded on him and snapped, "Seriously, could you stop laughing at me? I feel ridiculous enough already in this costume."

Nick blinked in surprise. "I wasn't." He

dropped his gaze over Hunter's body. Yes, the costume was comical, but those lean legs were enticing in the tights, and the way the green jacket just skimmed the bulge of Hunter's package… "There's nothing wrong with the way you look." He'd meant it to be reassuring, but it had come out decidedly flirty.

But Hunter rolled his eyes, his arms crossed tightly. "Yeah, right. Now you're just messing with me."

He bit back a surge of irritation. This was exactly why Nick spent most of his time with his trees and his dog. People were so much damn work. He clamped down on his urge to soothe. "If you say so."

"I just…" Hunter clenched his jaw. "Forget it." He swiped off his hat with attached ears, running a hand through his damp hair, sweat glistening on his forehead. "Jesus, it's hot out there."

"That we can agree on." Nick tried to unfasten the long beard, which fit with a string around his head that hooked together at the side, but the hook seemed to be caught in his hat by his ear. He tugged, but it was no use. "Can you give me a hand?"

After a beat of silence, Hunter pointed to himself and asked, "Me?"

"I don't see any other elves here." He motioned to his ear. "The hook's caught."

"Oh. Right. Um…" Hunter neared as if he was afraid Nick would bite.

And goddamn if that didn't rattle the cage of Nick's inner dom.

Tentatively, Hunter tugged on the snag, his knuckles brushing the corner of Nick's jaw. Nick watched from the corner of his eye as Hunter frowned and said, "It's really tangled somehow." He leaned closer, going up on his tip-toes, the bells on his shoes dinging softly. He wavered, and Nick took hold of Hunter's waist with one hand to steady him.

Hunter sucked in a breath, a tremor rippling through the firm muscles under Nick's palm. "These shoes are too tight," he mumbled. "Hard to get my balance."

"Take your time." Nick spread his fingers, wondering what Hunter's body would feel like naked.

Hunter stuck out the pink tip of his tongue as he concentrated on the hook. "There." He lifted off the hat, and the beard mercifully came free as he stepped back and Nick let go of him.

The fake beard made his real hair itchy, and Nick rubbed at his face. "Thanks." He unbuckled the thick black belt and dropped it to the concrete floor with a thud before stripping off his coat and padding. His white tank top stuck to his skin, and goosebumps spread over him in the chill of the room compared to the heat out in the mall. He tugged at the scooped neck of the cotton, tempted to peel it off, but he'd only have to put it back on damp.

When he looked up, a new shiver ran through him—one that had nothing to do with the temperature. Hunter was staring at Nick's chest, his full lips parted, a shine glistening as if he'd just licked them. He jerked his gaze up to Nick's, his Adam's apple bobbing. "Oh, um… You're welcome." He spun away with a decidedly guilty expression on his pretty face to go along with the lust.

Despite himself, Nick's balls tingled, and as John opened the door, Nick found himself flushing as well even though nothing had happened. Hunter stared at his feet, and silence stretched out. Holding a bulging paper bag and cardboard cup holder, John looked between them with arched eyebrows.

"How are my Santa and elf holding up?"

They nodded and assured him they were great, and the three of them sat on overturned crates, John fortunately carrying the conversation as they ate, telling them all about the plans for Toys and Turkeys.

After Hunter excused himself to go to the

washroom, Nick asked, "What's his story?" before he could stop himself, barely even waiting for the door to shut. He huffed at himself in his mind. He did not have time to give a shit about anything but his harvest, and here he was in a Santa suit finding himself intrigued by a mall elf half his age.

John sucked cola through a straw. "Hunter's a good kid. Single mother. His father took off when he was a baby, I think. His mom's Pam Adams; she's a nurse at County. Probably knew Eric, come to think of it. Hunter worked for me when he was in high school. Went to U of T and graduated last year, but I think he's having trouble getting a job. Seems like he's floundering."

"Probably because this generation expects trophies just for showing up."

"Always the cynic." John shook his head with a mix of exasperation and affection. "It's not so easy for them, you know. Cost of living keeps going up, but salaries sure don't. It was easier for our parents, harder for us, and harder still for them. There aren't the jobs there used to be, at least not for decent money."

"Fair point." Nick popped a fry into his mouth, savoring the salty grease.

"I was reading about how new lawyers have to take the paralegal jobs because they can't find anything else. I wouldn't want to be starting work now, I tell you." He motioned with a fry. "But you know, I'm glad at least it's better for them coming out. Hunter did it when he was seventeen, which still wasn't *easy* in Pinevale. Took courage. He's always been high-strung, and he was pretty shy back then; I don't think he had a lot of friends."

"Really? With that face?" *And that ass?* Despite himself, Nick imagined the lovely *smack* his palm would make against that perky backside. Eric's teasing voice filled his mind.

Well, you do think today's youth needs more discipline.

John smiled slyly. "You like what you see, eh? I thought so."

"What? No." Nick scoffed. "He's half my age."

"And? As you can see, he's all grown up now. Back then he was covered in zits. Very awkward. He's still self-conscious, I think, despite looking like he does. Not that I would look."

Nick laughed. "You're married, not dead. I'm sure Des looks too."

John chuckled. "Yep. Do you ever watch that *Riverdale*? Archie is much more attractive than he should be."

"I've seen it listed on Netflix. I'll check it

out."

"Netflix? So you mean you don't just sit around out there in the woods brooding and writing poetry and other Byronic pursuits?"

Nick tossed his wadded-up napkin at him, trying not to smile. "Shut up."

"But really, you're out there alone so much of the time. You really are becoming a hermit, and you're only, what? Forty-six? Are you hooking up, at least?"

"Sure, once in a while." Nick shrugged. "I go to the club in Barrie. It's fine." It had gotten a little boring, if he was honest. In a rural area, pickings were slim, and he hadn't found anyone who wanted a daddy or whose needs could satisfy him. Although he and Eric had only been five years apart in age, Nick had definitely been Daddy in the bedroom, and they'd both found it incredibly fulfilling.

But Nick hadn't assumed the role in years now. For him it was about more than just play-acting—the satisfaction came in that genuine need and surrender, giving them both peace. In his sporadic hookups over the years, he'd never met anyone with that certain vulnerability he was drawn to. Maybe he should have tried harder to meet more men, but it was so much damn work. Simpler to lose himself in the solitude and dependable rhythms of the farm.

"And do you ever bring someone out there to the Fortress of Solitude?"

Nick ate another fry. "You and Des come for dinner every month"

"We don't count."

He shrugged. "I have a dog. She's much better company than people."

"As wonderful as Ella is, she does lack certain qualities that people possess."

"I know. That's why she's perfect when she's not chasing squirrels and getting sprayed by skunks. But you'll be delighted to hear that I'm going to have to hire an extra hand to cut down trees this week. The demand is late this season after that warm spell at the beginning of December. I'll be behind after taking time out to play Santa."

John grimaced. "I'm sorry to put you out. I really do appreciate you stepping up at the last minute—especially considering how much you hate people, and particularly crowds of them." John winked, but his smile faded. "And I don't mean to nag. We worry about you all alone out there as the years go by. We just wish—"

Hunter returned, skidding to a halt as John and Nick looked at him. In the silence, he fidgeted and defensively asked, "What?"

Such rough, skittish edges Hunter had, and Nick wondered what it would take to calm those jitters. Which was *ridiculous.* He had no time to be intrigued by some pretty young man, so he said dryly, "Don't worry, we weren't talking about you." He looked away dismissively.

"Actually, you're just the man Nick needs!" John clapped his hands, grinning. "He was saying he needs help on the farm next week, and I know you're looking for more work. It's the perfect solution."

Nick glared at him, not sure whether the bolt of adrenaline coursing through him was dread or anticipation. "I was going to ask Bill Chang."

"I think he's in Florida," John said. "Hunter, you're free during the week, right?"

Hunter eyed Nick uneasily. "Yeah, totally. Uh, what kind of work is it?"

John said, "Nick owns a Christmas tree farm. Off ninety-three, out near Thorny Creek. All by his lonesome." To Nick, he asked, "You need help chopping down and that kind of stuff?"

Well... Maybe there was no harm in giving the kid a chance. "Yes. It's hard, sweaty work— and not the kind from wearing silly costumes in an overheated mall." He'd meant it as a joke, but Hunter shifted from foot to foot, crossing his arms. Not defiantly—defensively.

Hunter said, "Oh, okay. I don't know if I'm strong enough?"

The urge to guide and show him just how strong he could be rose up in Nick, a hunger he knew he should ignore. "If you don't think you can do it, I'll find someone else." He shrugged carelessly, yet he hoped Hunter would meet the challenge.

Yes, there was something about him—the spirited insolence paired with uneasiness, that self-consciousness like he truly didn't realize how beautiful he was. He seemed to be a jumble of contradictions, but Nick supposed he was too. He found most people exhausting and preferred solitude, yet he was drawn to Hunter.

"I can do it." Hunter nodded as if convincing himself, drawing up straighter, his tights leaving nothing to the imagination. "Definitely."

"There you go!" John opened a box of doughnut holes and ate one with gusto. "Santa and his elf! What could be better?"

Chapter Three

*O*MG *IS IT true you're back in the tights???*

Hunter smiled as Shelby's text flashed on his phone's screen Monday night, and he paused his game and stretched out on his mom's old leather couch. Shelby had been one of his few friends in high school and a fellow mall elf back when John could afford to hire more than one.

Hunter wished desperately that she was still in Pinevale, or at least Ontario. She'd gone to UBC and had landed a job at a hip yoga company in Vancouver. He was thrilled for her, of course. Maybe a little jealous that she seemed to have her life figured out, but at least ninety-five percent thrilled.

He typed back:

I hope my temporary return to elfhood isn't the biggest news Pinevale's gossip network has to offer.

Shelby responded:

I'm afraid so. Although I also hear Santa's some super hottie? Do tell. And poor Mr. Tremblay. He was always so nice.

Hunter filled her in on what he knew about Mr. Tremblay and his broken hip. Then he added:

Santa was hot, yeah. He owns some Christmas tree farm way out of town? He was kind of a dick, tbh.

Which hadn't stopped Hunter from seeing visions of Nick's chest in that white undershirt, his chest hair poking out, arms thick, nipples so…lickable.

OMFG, that hot guy who lives in the woods? I met him once when my mom went to talk to him about getting trees to sell for the Girl Guides. I was only thirteen or something, but I definitely appreciated that whole lumberjack vibe.

Hunter replied:

Yeah, he's still got that going on. He waited for Shelby's response.

You know, I think he might be gay now that I think about it? You should get on that. Tell him you've been very, very naughty.

He sucked in a breath, excitement sparking. Nick was gay? Well, he was apparently friends with John—not that John didn't have straight friends. But it was irrelevant anyway. Hunter laughed out loud and said to himself, "Even if Nick Spini's gay, he thinks I'm an idiot. And even if he didn't, I'd never get a guy like that." Before he could respond to Shelby, she sent:

And don't give me that crap about you not being hot enough. It's like you look in the mirror and still see yourself in grade ten. You're gorgeous. You realize most dudes are totally intimidated by you, right? And this is why you're somehow still a virgin despite being a walking wet dream?

Hunter barked out a laugh and replied:

Sure. If you say so.

He could imagine her impatient huff as she typed:

I'm telling you. Remember when we went out last summer when I came home? I know you're nervous and insecure, but it comes across like you're not interested. So you go home alone when everyone in the bar wants to bang you. Also, I maintain that Brett Leblanc wanted to do you even though you were still in your awkward phase.

He winced thinking of star hockey player Brett, who'd teased him and called him gay so much that Hunter had finally stood up to him and said he was, and if Brett didn't like it, he could kiss his queer ass. That had amazingly shut up Brett and anyone else who might have had an issue with it.

Hunter had already been honest about his

sexuality at home, but he'd never planned to come out at school. It had turned out shockingly okay. He wished he could bottle the confidence he'd had in that moment and apply it to the rest of his life. Maybe he just needed to get really angry for it to come out. So to speak.

Seriously, you're a babe. It's time you got out of your own way. And don't roll your eyes.

Laughing, he stopped himself, although his eyes were halfway there. He typed:

Okay, okay, I'm gorgeous. Now fill me in about that new guy you're seeing.

He didn't tell Shelby he was going to Nick's farm the next day to work. It would probably be a disaster, and he didn't want to have to tell her later that he'd failed. Every time he'd had a job interview and had been sure he'd get it, having to tell Shelby and his family that he hadn't gotten the job after all had been more and more embarrassing.

After they finished texting, Hunter put down his phone and watched the lights on the fake tree in the corner of the living room shine on the glittery ornaments. He said out loud, "I'm gorgeous," then scoffed.

He was fine. Not too short, a little skinny, but not as bad as he used to be. His face had cleared up aside from the freckle situation, and he had okay blond hair. He'd definitely planned on having so much sex in university, but he'd always held back for some reason. He'd never been able to really let go and trust another guy, and then he'd started to feel extremely self-conscious about still being a virgin. Now here he was caught in a vicious cycle.

He closed his eyes, letting one of his favorite fantasies unspool. It was only images, really—a beefy man being in charge, Hunter being penetrated hard or maybe even spanked. All the control and worry taken from him so he could relax and be free. Be fucked and taken care of. He'd watched plenty of porn, and he was always drawn to the hairy doms.

His cock stirred, and he rubbed it with the heel of his hand through his track pants. In his fantasies, the man taking control was always older, although Hunter had never had the guts to try it in real life. He was terrified he'd be laughed at, and he'd probably get it all stupidly wrong anyway due to the whole virgin thing.

He should just man up, install Grindr, find some guy, and get his first time over with. Rip off the Band-Aid. It wasn't like he didn't *want* to have sex, but he'd built it into a mountain in his mind. He'd been too chickenshit to put himself out there for too long.

The idea that Nick was gay popped back

into Hunter's head. On Sunday, they'd done another long day in Santa's Village, and Nick hadn't said much aside from giving him gruff instructions on coming out to the farm on Tuesday. But Hunter could have sworn he'd caught Nick checking out his ass more than once. That he'd felt…*something* in the air between them in that freezing storage room. He'd clearly made a shitty first impression on Nick by being late, and he was determined to prove himself.

He laughed out loud, shaking his head. Nick probably couldn't have cared less, and it was all in Hunter's pathetic virgin mind. Still, his thoughts drifted back to Nick. *Was* he gay? Had he actually been checking out Hunter's ass?

He was probably staring because I looked so stupid and lame in that costume.

But there was nothing wrong with playing what-if, was there? He shifted on the couch, the leather squeaking. Hunter imagined Nick with other guys, and he was going to be full-on jerking off in a minute. If Nick was gay, did he have a boyfriend? Husband?

Would he go for a younger guy?

Hunter's breath caught, and he shoved his hand into his track pants, gripping his cock as the floodgates opened and the fantasy took over. He imagined himself over Nick's knee on that bench in the mall, getting spanked as he cried out, Nick totally in control, holding him down, not letting him wriggle, showing him how to do everything—

The engine of his mom's Ford Focus rattled as she pulled into the driveway, the garage door vibrating as it rolled up. Hunter shot to his feet, turning in a circle before he sat back down, grabbed a throw cushion and plonked it on his lap, and picked up the game controller. He started playing, the sound of battle hopefully drowning out his panting.

"Hi, sweetie!" his mom called as she opened the door.

From where he was on the couch in the living room at the front of the house, he couldn't see her yet in the foyer, but he could feel the blast of arctic air. "Hey!"

She stuck her head around the corner and pulled off her toque, a dusting of snow falling to the tiles. Her hair was blond like his, and it was coming out of the bun she wore for work. "Did you have a good day?"

"Uh-huh. I made dinner. It probably sucks."

She pursed her lips. "I was just going to ask what that wonderful smell was. I'm sure it'll be delicious, and thank you." She took off her coat and boots, her purple scrubs wrinkled under-neath. "I'm going to have a quick shower." She glanced at the TV. "Are you winning?"

He'd just gotten seriously injured because he was paying more attention to his mercifully flagging boner, but Hunter nodded and gave her a smile before she disappeared down the hallway toward the bedrooms. Their single-level house had three bedrooms and two bathrooms, and a finished basement that was mostly used for storage now that Heather and Hunter had (mostly) moved out. There was a nice little yard out back with a corner vegetable garden in summer. It was home.

In the beige kitchen, the worn linoleum chilly under his bare feet, he stirred the chili in the slow cooker, inhaling the cumin and other spices. It wasn't fancy, but it hit the spot. He turned on the oven to heat up the crusty bread. The kitchen wallpaper was a rooster design, and every time his mom watched HGTV, she talked about tearing out the old brown cupboards and doing a back-splash and new flooring and an island. But while she was lending Hunter money to make his monthly student loan payments, she couldn't afford it.

His stomach tightened. He'd been so sure he'd be able to find some kind of job during the six-month grace period for loans after graduation. He'd worked serving tables all through university, but it had been too much with the long hours the internships had demanded and commuting to his sister's condo in suburban Mississauga.

At least the companies had paid his transit expenses, which they'd made seem very generous. Hunter was willing to pay his dues, but at a certain point he needed actual freaking money.

"I can hear you worrying from down the hall," his mom said as she entered the kitchen, her slippers flapping on the tile. Her flannel PJs were covered in sleeping cats, and her wet hair hung over her shoulders. She kissed his cheek. "Don't worry, be happy."

"Are you going to start whistling that song?"

She twisted the top off a bottle of red and pulled down two glasses. "Probably." She handed him a glass. "Vino for your thoughts."

He took it and sipped the oaky, spicy wine. "The usual. That I can't get a real job, and I'm going to end up living in your basement until you kick me out."

"Good thing I'd never kick you out." She winked, the lines around her eyes crinkling as she smiled. She was fifty now but still super pretty. Hunter's father was a douchebag and moron for leaving her since she was the best. Hunter had been a baby when his father took off, but they'd been well rid of him. She'd dated a bit over the years but said she was single and happy now.

Still, Hunter couldn't help but feel guilty that both he and his older sister had moved out. Was his mom lonely here on her own? She never complained about it, but then again, she'd never let him hear her complain about anything that mattered.

"And your sister won't kick you out either, for the record."

He sighed. "I know, but… It's bad enough I've been freeloading off Heather since I graduated. She and Rick have been amazing, but they have the baby now. She doesn't want her little brother taking up the room that's supposed to be the baby's. It's not fair that they have to have the crib and everything in their room. I can't go back in the new year. I need to find another place. Give up on landing a real job and go back to waiting tables. I made good money."

"Mmm." She sipped her wine, leaning back against the counter. "You talk a lot about getting a 'real' job. Is being a server not a real job?"

"No, of course it is. I just mean, like…" He

rubbed his face. "After university, you're supposed to get, like, a *grown-up* job. A career."

"And you want your career to be in marketing and communications?"

He shrugged. "I have an English degree, and I can write. I don't want to go to teacher's college because the only reason I'd want to teach is to get summers off, and that's a shitty reason. So if I want to work in business, communications makes sense."

"But do you want to work in business?"

He shrugged again. "I want to make a decent salary one day. It doesn't feel like there are a lot of options. I don't love working in an office, but most people don't, right?"

She sipped her wine and took bowls from the creaky cabinet. "Do you have to work in an office to have a 'real' job?"

"Well, it depends. Obviously you work in the hospital, and that's a real career. But what am I going to do with an English lit degree if I'm not working in some kind of office?"

"Do you have to *do* something with it? Is it not valuable in and of itself?"

Hunter stuck his hand in an oven mitt, flinching from the wave of heat as he took out the bread and dropped it on the cutting board. "You're very philosophical tonight."

"I am, aren't I?" She laughed and pulled

him into a hug. "Just give it some thought. You realize there are plenty of people older than you who are still living with their parents and have no idea what to do with their lives, right? It's common these days." She pulled back with a frown. "But you're always so hard on yourself. And unpaid internships should be illegal."

He shrugged. "They're supposed to be, but the companies find loopholes. If you complain, you can guess who's *not* getting a job there in the end."

"It's BS, is what it is. You've more than paid your dues. So don't stress, honey. It's the holidays. You'll figure it all out."

When? What if I don't?

Hunter nodded and smiled, shoving away the worry. "You're right."

"Always." She winked.

They ate in front of the TV as usual, watching a recording of whatever procedural had been on recently. As his mom fast-forwarded through commercials, she asked, "So what's this job you lined up for tomorrow?"

Lust flamed through him thinking of his little fantasy earlier, and Hunter took a mouthful of chili and shrugged. But she paused the TV and waited for him to swallow. He cleared his throat. "I'm helping at a Christmas tree farm. The guy's a friend of John's? Nick

Spini."

"Oh! Nick." She smiled. "Huh. I haven't heard that name in years."

His heart skipped. "You know him?"

"No, not really. I worked with his partner, though. Dr. McKinnon. Eric." Her smile went sad and distant. "Such a lovely man. Always had a smile for you even after a double shift. It was incredibly tragic, what happened."

Hunter toyed with his spoon, his chest tightening. "What happened?"

She stared off into the distance. "A boy fell through the ice on Swiss Lake, and Eric was driving by. He stopped and tried to save him, of course. Called 911 before he went onto the lake, but more of the ice gave way, and the water was just too cold. They'd both drowned by the time police arrived."

"Wow." So Nick *was* indeed gay or bi or whatever, but Hunter couldn't feel happy about it after hearing *that*.

"Nick was devastated, as you can imagine. He disappeared, more or less. I actually forgot about him." Tears glistened in her eyes, and she shook her head, focusing on Hunter again. "Isn't that sad?"

"It's not your fault. When did it happen?"

She swiped at her eyes. "Let me think." After a few moments, she said, "Must be seven or eight years ago now. Yes, eight, I think." A tear slipped down her cheek. "Poor Nick. How could I have not thought of him at all in so long?"

"From what I gather, he's kind of a hermit out there with his trees?" Hunter slid closer on the couch, putting his arm around her shoulders. "It's okay. Please don't cry."

Sniffing loudly, she half-laughed. "Oh, don't mind me. I swear, these hormones are making me an emotional wreck these days. Peri-menopause needs to shove it. Hard."

Laughing, he kissed her cheek and inhaled the fresh scent of her herbal shampoo. "Those hormones don't know who they're messing with." He paused, then added, "I love you, Mom."

"Well, aren't we just a couple of saps to-night? Thank you, honey. You know I love you too." She patted his knee. "And I'm so glad to hear you'll be spending time with Nick."

"Yeah. Hopefully it'll be okay? He's not much of a people person, I guess. But John got him to fill in as Santa, and he was actually really sweet with the kids." It had been incredibly sexy seeing him listening to the kids like their requests were all he cared about when Hunter knew he was probably bored shitless. "He said to come tomorrow since he needed today to be alone. You're sure it's cool for me to take the car on your day off?"

"Yep. I'm doing nothing tomorrow but reading my romance and relaxing. The duke is about to realize that the new stable boy is actually a young woman on the run from a dastardly viscount."

"Ohh, the plot thickens. Has he been confusingly attracted to this stable boy?"

She laughed. "Indeed he has."

"Good times."

"How about another glass of wine while we finish our dinner? Which is delicious, by the way. And don't say it was easy and shrug off the compliment. It's *delicious*. Thank you for making it. Now go get me more wine."

Hunter grinned. "Yes, ma'am."

He poured himself another glass too since it was still early. Later that night, he was going to set three alarms and make sure he was at Nick's bright and early and ready to impress. And he was *totally* going to jerk off to fantasies of sitting on Nick's lap and being very, very naughty.

"NO, NO, NO!"

The tires couldn't grip the hidden patch of

ice, and as the road curved, there was nothing Hunter could do but cling to the steering wheel and brace as he slid into the ditch.

His heart pounded in his ears as he jolted to a stop, the car now tilted alarmingly, passenger side down and lodged deep in a snowdrift. The seat belt dug into the side of his neck. For a few frantic breaths, he didn't move. At least the airbag hadn't gone off and punched him in the face.

An old Bryan Adams song about Christmastime blared from the radio, and Hunter jabbed it off with a trembling finger, muttering, "Yeah, not so much magic in the air right now. But I'm okay." His voice was thin and unconvincing. He moved his limbs, and nothing seemed broken. He might have a few bruises from the seat belt, but nothing major.

"I'm okay," he repeated. And now he was stuck in a ditch in the middle of nowhere, and he was going to be late. "Fucking fuck!" He pounded the steering wheel, his leather gloves muffling the blows.

It was still dark, and he'd never been on the route that led to Nick's farm. The headlights illuminated more snow falling amid the shadowy trees looming around him, the narrow road curving out of sight. In the rear view, the high snow bank he was stuck in glowed a ghostly red above his taillights, only a void beyond. He panted harshly, twitching with the lingering adrenaline spiking through him.

Driving out toward Nick's, he hadn't even seen another vehicle in the last half an hour. He'd turned off the paved county road at least fifteen minutes ago, and Nick's driveway, which seemed pretty long on Hunter's navigation app, should have been within a couple kilometers. He grabbed his phone from the holder attached to the dashboard and blinked at the screen, the red band at the top sending a bolt of icy panic through him.

Searching for signal

"No! You have to have a signal!" He shook the phone, as if that would help somehow. "Fuck!" Gripping the phone, he closed his eyes, trying to breathe.

He was leaning down to the right, and if not for the seat belt holding him in place, he would have crashed into the passenger side when the car had slid into the ditch. But maybe if he gunned the engine, he'd be able to drive up and out? Highly unlikely, but he had to try.

"Okay. Come on, Jacques. You can do it." His mom had ironically named her car after an old Canadian racecar driver, and Hunter called on every spirit of Christmas and racecar drivers and justice in the universe as he eased on the accelerator, letting the tires grip before he gave it more gas.

The car shuddered and moved about an inch, the engine revving and the tires spinning uselessly.

"Damn it, Jacques!" He pounded the steering wheel and closed his eyes, wishing more than anything that this was a terrible dream. He muttered to himself, "Okay, think. You can handle this." He laughed harshly. "You *have* to handle this."

He opened his eyes and turned off the engine, silence setting in. First he had to call Nick to let him know he'd be late. Cringing, Hunter remembered Nick's sneer when he'd shown up late that first morning. That had totally been his fault, but this wasn't!

Surely Nick would understand. He was grumpy and gruff, but he'd been sweet with the kids, and John and his husband were friends with him. It was horrible what happened to his partner, and Nick was probably a great guy.

He'd understand.

Hunter tapped his screen with the special touch pad of his glove, acid flooding his stomach as he stared at the complete absence of bars. His voice sounded high and tight as he talked to himself. "Okay, I'll get out, and I'll find a signal. It's fine."

He shoved his door open, pushing against gravity. Bracing himself, he undid his seat belt, grunting as he climbed out. His side of the car was pointed up, and he had to jump down a couple feet to the ground, his boots sinking into the fresh snow up to his knees, his jeans instantly wet. Fuck, he should have worn his snow pants.

Dumbass!

There had been a bit of snow falling in town when he'd woken, but nothing remarkable. He should have known the farm would be in the snow-belt. It was amazing how the wind patterns, presence or absence of lakes, and the rise and fall of the land meant there'd be a couple inches of snow in one area and three times that not far away. His weather app had called for more snow later in the day, but it was falling heavier and heavier, the blowing wind reducing visibility.

Hunter held up his phone, walking in a circle through the growing drifts of snow. It was still dark as midnight, and his phone glowed in the gloom. He stood in the middle of the road, joy seizing him as a bar appeared.

"Yes, yes!" He jabbed at the screen, opening his contacts, where he'd put Nick's number in under "Santa Nick." He connected, putting the phone to his ear. His hat was in the car, and he brushed thick snow from his hair, his ears already stinging. The base temperature was actually not far below freezing—perfect conditions for damp, snowman-making snow—but the windchill was killer.

"Hello?" Nick answered.

"Hi!" Hunter's pulse raced. "I'm so sorry. I'm going to be late."

There was a huff of irritation. "It's six-fifty-two. You have eight minutes."

Humiliation ripped through him, and Hunter felt small and stupid even though he wanted to argue that he wasn't that far away and he would have been there on time, if not early despite the unexpected conditions. "I'm sorry. It's just that—"

"It doesn't matter. This was a mistake. Don't bother coming."

"Wait! I—this—" Hunter tripped over his words. "Let me explain. My car's in the ditch."

Silence.

Blood rushed in Hunter's ears. "Hello?"

Nothing.

Jerking the phone away from his ear, he stared at the home screen. The single bar was still there. Had Nick actually *hung up* on him? "Are you serious right now?" he yelled at his phone. He wasn't sure if he was more furious or hurt. He shouldn't have cared if Nick liked him or wanted his approval, but…he did. Which was pathetic.

After pacing back and forth, he stopped and inhaled deeply. It hadn't been nostril-hair-freezing cold out when he'd left, but the wind was whipping up steadily as a storm apparently moved in. "Okay. Mom has CAA. Just have to call them. No problem."

He heaved open the car door, bracing himself on one knee so he could lean in and reach the glove box. He was blocking the overhead light, and he rooted around, feeling for the thick plastic folder. When he had it, he grabbed his wool hat and scarf, crawled back out, and closed the door. "Okay, emergency assistance," he mumbled, programming the number into his phone and saving it. "Here we go."

As soon as he got a signal again.

After fifteen minutes of slogging up and down the road, keeping the car in sight while jumping, praying, and waving his phone around, Hunter had to declare defeat. The sun was coming up for what it was worth—which wasn't much in the gloom of the forest, the wind definitely awakened and bringing down the temperature. The blowing snow stung Hunter's cheeks and eyes, his nose icy.

Back in the car, he belted himself in and turned on the engine to warm up and think for a minute. He rubbed his hands briskly in his gloves, waiting for the heat to kick in. Someone was bound to come along. He wasn't *that* far from civilization. Surely other people lived down this road, not just Nick. He hadn't seen any tire tracks in the snow, but that didn't mean anything. People would be going to work and coming along.

Definitely.

He jabbed at the radio, switching it to the local news station. The announcer's voice filled the car, her tone serious. "—snow squall warning is in effect, with the forecasted weather activity arriving hours earlier than expected and with far greater intensity, including winds gusting over seventy kilometers an hour by late morning. The OPP warn that they expect to enforce road closures on several routes in the area, including—"

Hunter's heart sank as she listed off road names, including the main county road he'd turned off. The odds of anyone coming along would plummet along with the visibility. "Fuck me," he muttered, fear beginning to drag icy fingers down his spine.

The vents had started shooting warm air, and Hunter peeled off his gloves and held up his bare hands. At least he wouldn't freeze if he had the engine on sporadically—

Gasping with a burst of true panic, he twisted off the ignition and shoved at the door to get out. He stumbled to the ground, scrabbling around to get his footing, his hands still bare. Another patch of hidden ice sent him sprawling flat out, heavy snow in his face. He finally got to his hands and knees, then to his feet, his legs shaking.

He peered around the back of the car, and sure enough, the tailpipe was completely stuck in the snowbank and blocked.

"Yeah, getting carbon monoxide poisoning is not going to help," he muttered to himself, remembering the story he saw on the news about how deadly gas could build up in a snow-bound car in under two minutes with the engine on. A mother and kids had died the previous winter, and it had happened crazy fast.

Pulse galloping, he inhaled the cold air deeply, jamming his fists in the pockets of his ski jacket. He felt okay—not sleepy or con-fused. He hadn't smelled any gas in the car, but of course carbon monoxide was odorless, so that didn't mean jack shit.

Would I even know if I'm confused? Am I thinking clearly?

He kept breathing deeply, turning his back to the wind and leaving the door open to air out the car. When he was as certain as he could be that he was in his right mind—the decision to come work for Nick Spini notwithstanding—Hunter opened the trunk, snow from the drift up to his waist.

There was cat litter to help the tires grip, a first aid kit, some bungee cords, the spare tire and jack, and a wool blanket. No shovel, so he couldn't dig out the car. He pulled out the blanket and wrapped it around his shoulders before going back into the front seat, sitting there for a minute out of the wind.

He tried to get a signal again, but it was no use. Even if he was strong enough to push the car out of the ditch, he needed someone behind the wheel putting on the gas. The only way Jacques was getting free was probably with a tow truck. Hunter climbed out, the thud of the door closing muffled in the snow.

It was silent in the trees aside from the growing howl of the wind and his own harsh breathing. What if he sat in the freezing car and no one came? He'd be out of the wind, but...

Hunter peered down the empty road behind and in front of him and listened, holding his breath. Nothing. No distant engines. No signs of rescue. He hadn't passed anything on his way from the county road, and it was a hell of a long walk, especially if the county road would be closed. Nick's farm had to be closer.

It was the last place Hunter wanted to go, but it was preferable to freezing to death.

"I can't believe that asshole hung up on me," he announced to the forest. "Asshole!"

His shout was lost on the wind. The fact that he actually was in danger of freezing was an icy fist in his chest, and he had to keep panic at bay. He could follow the road and hope Nick's drive had a sign. At least he'd be doing something instead of just waiting and hoping.

Because what if no one came by for hours? It was very possible no one would. If he waited and *then* made a try for Nick's, he'd be in worse shape and trapped in even more snow. No, he couldn't just sit there.

The car alarm made a cheery little chirp as he pressed the lock button, leaving Jacques behind as he trudged toward what he hoped was the lesser of two evils.

Chapter Four

"**E**LLA, LEAVE THE damn squirrels alone!" Nick shouted into the wind as she barked. Visibility was crap, but that was beagles for you. Her nose could whiff out a squirrel, skunk, or raccoon kilometers away even if she couldn't see them. She always seemed disappointed when Nick didn't want to hunt them with her. At least they didn't have many bears around this far south, although a few had been spotted that summer.

He pushed up the fuzzy brim of his red trapper hat, which attached under his chin and protected his cheeks. He couldn't see anything beyond twenty feet in front of him. The weatherman hadn't called for a damn blizzard, but those fools were always wrong—especially with global warming making the weather more unpredictable than Nick could ever remember it. But blizzard or no blizzard, he had to harvest.

He fired up the chainsaw again, felling another tree from the grid of six- and seven-foot Fraser firs that were ready for market. Picking up the tree with his thick gloves, he shook it to get rid of any dead needles, his muscles aching already, and it wasn't even ten a.m.

Nick hefted the tree over to the baler, the engine on the round, red machine still running under the tarp he'd strung. He fed the tree into the baler's mouth, and it came out the other side wrapped in twine and ready to be stacked.

Ella was still barking at something back toward the house, her smallish brown-and-white body tense. Nick squinted through the snow. They were in the first acre closest to home, not far along the access road. He'd have to plow again with the pickup before he could get the flatbed truck down to load the trees, and the way the storm had taken hold, it would probably be tomorrow. He was used to doing everything himself—regularly working fourteen-hour days from spring through to Christmas—but it would have been good to have another pair of hands.

Too bad the sexy elf had proved unreliable after all.

He laughed at his foolishness. *Sexy elf.* Nick

should have known better than to ever agree to hire him. Showing up late was apparently his MO, and Nick had zero tolerance for that shit, snow or no snow. Hunter should have left earlier and made sure he made it by seven a.m. sharp.

Nick should have known not to…what? Get his hopes up? He grunted, scowling to himself. He was better off on his own, and he'd just have to work harder. He'd already shipped out thousands of trees, but demand was high now around the fifteenth of December as busy people hurried to play catch-up and get their trees. The local nursery had asked for more than usual. Why had he agreed to play Santa and waste so much time?

"Yes, I'm being a grouch, Eric," he said to the trees, his words swallowed by the wind. He wasn't in the mood to hear the echo of Eric's teasing in his mind.

Ella had gone farther back up the access road, and her barking grew more agitated. Nick squinted again but couldn't see anything, Ella disappearing. Instinct told him it wasn't a squirrel or skunk, so he whistled for her and turned off the baler, covering it completely.

Letting Ella in first, he climbed into the pickup, driving slowly through the wall of white, the plow attached to the front of the truck clearing the way. As he neared the house, a dark smudge appeared, and he slammed on the brakes, the pickup jolting.

"Who the hell—" His heart skipped. It had to be Hunter, and Nick couldn't fight the pulse of eagerness at seeing him again. He realized he was smiling, for fuck's sake. With a grumble at himself, he wiped his expression blank. He'd told Hunter not to come, and that should have been the end of it. This was a distraction he didn't need.

He climbed out, Ella racing ahead, and called, "I told you to forget it!" before stomping over. "Why—" He halted a few feet from Hunter, blinking at him, Ella nosing around Hunter's knees.

Hunter was covered in snow. It topped the pom-pom on his dark woolen toque and the blanket wrapped around him, and dusted across his red, wind-raw face, his eyelashes actually white. He shook, his teeth chattering.

Nick looked beyond him and asked, "Where's your car?"

"In a ditch a few kilometers before the turnoff for your road." Hunter's voice was thin in the howling wind, his breathing labored. "I tried to tell you, but you hung up on me."

Fuck.

Despite the wind's bitter chill, shame and

pure disgust at himself heated Nick's face and neck, bile in his throat. It was true—he had hung up before Hunter could explain his lateness. Christ, that had been hours ago! In the snow squalls, Hunter could have easily lost his way and frozen out there. Hell, he looked close to it now. Nick knew better than most how quickly nature could be fatal.

Shoving away the jagged, razor-sharp memories, he asked, "Are you hurt?" He took hold of Hunter's arms as if he'd be able to feel injuries.

Hunter shook his head. "Sorry to bug you. The OPP is closing roads, and I kept trying to get a signal, but it won't connect."

Nick shepherded him to the house. "Don't be sorry. Come on."

Inside, Nick flipped on the overhead light. Usually the big window in the open living room and the kitchen window off to the right beyond the little foyer and closet provided plenty of natural light, but in the blizzard, the house was dim. It did feel warm, at least, even though Nick kept the thermostat low and hadn't lit a fire yet.

On the wide mat inside the front door, he eased the snow-crusted blanket from around Hunter, who shivered. Nick tossed his own heavy work gloves and hat into the corner and tried to shoo away Ella, who lingered curiously, sniffing their rare guest eagerly as Hunter toed off his boots before easing free his gloves and snow-crusted hat and scarf. His fingers trembled as he pet Ella's head, and then he struggled with the zipper of his ski jacket.

"Here." Nick unzipped it for him and pulled it free of Hunter's arms, hanging it on a wall hook. Damn it, he should have listened when Hunter had called. He'd been far angrier than the situation called for, and now guilt clawed at him. He yanked off his own boots, then his waterproof pants and jacket, and the fleece he'd layered over a plaid flannel shirt and thermal work pants. "How long have you been here? Why didn't you come inside right away?"

Hunter only watched him warily, shuddering, hugging himself.

Nick realized he'd sort-of *yelled* the questions. He cleared his throat and added more calmly, "I just mean that it wasn't locked. I would have wanted you to come in."

Ella pushed eagerly against Hunter's legs, and Nick snapped his fingers and pointed to her dog bed in the kitchen corner. "Ella, go. Now." With a single bark of protest, she did.

"I thought you'd probably kill me if I broke into your house," Hunter whispered hoarsely, his teeth clacking.

More shame flowed through him, digging into corners with sharp teeth. Nick nodded. "I can see why you'd have that impression. Jesus, you're frozen. Are you sure you aren't hurt? You didn't hit your head?"

"No," he rasped. "I wasn't going fast." He added, "I know how to drive in the snow!" as if he was waiting for Nick to accuse him of recklessness.

"I'm sure you do. We have to around here, especially with storms like this blowing in with hardly any warning. Then when we do get warnings, there will only be a couple centimeters of snow and it's nothing."

Brow creased, Hunter looked up at Nick as if trying to figure out a puzzle. "Yeah."

"Let's get you warmed up." He thought of Eric's old first-aid lessons. "If you have hypothermia, warm water could bring on arrhythmia, so a hot shower's out."

He put a hand on Hunter's tense shoulder and guided him to the thick rug by the couch in the living room. The wooden house had been built in a rustic cabin/chalet style, with a vaulted ceiling and the second story hallway open along the back with a bedroom on each side. It was decorated simply, although Nick had splurged on the thick navy-blue rug in front of the stone fireplace.

He guided Hunter there and gazed down at him, suddenly aware of how small Hunter was. Yes, Hunter was shivering from the cold, but Nick suspected he was also cowering because Nick had been judgmental and cruel when he'd hung up on him.

Making an effort to soften his tone, Nick said, "Those jeans look wet. How's your sweater? You should take them off. I'll get you some other clothes. Hold on."

After a long moment, his eyes wide, Hunter nodded.

Nick dashed upstairs for a sweatshirt, flannel PJ bottoms, and thick socks. Hunter was shivering where he left him. Keeping his gaze averted, Nick helped him undress. The green sweater was damp around the collar and wrists, and any wetness was the enemy to warmth.

Nick lifted the soft material over Hunter's head, trying to ignore how deliciously red Hunter's nipples were. He knelt to tug off Hunter's socks, which were damp either from sweat or snow getting in the tops of his boots. Hunter grabbed Nick's shoulder to keep his balance, his hand shaking.

Peeling the cold, snow-wet denim down Hunter's legs, Nick's fingers brushed pale hair, and he wondered if the hair around Hunter's groin was as blond before forcing his focus back on first aid.

He left Hunter in his gray boxer-briefs, tearing his eyes away and helping him into too-big PJ bottoms and sweatshirt. He tugged the drawstring on the pajamas tight, knotting it so they'd stay on Hunter's slim hips.

He knelt with the soft, black wool socks. "Here you go."

Hunter held onto Nick's shoulder again, fingers sharp and trembling. Nick brushed his ankles as he pulled up the socks for him. He stood to grab the thick red fleece blanket folded on the back of the brown leather couch and wrapped it around Hunter's shaking shoulders.

"Are you thirsty?" Nick asked. At Hunter's nod, he went to the kitchen and poured a glass of room-temperature water from the pitcher on the counter. Ella whined softly, and she looked back at Hunter, clearly longing to meet him properly. Nick squatted and scratched behind her ears before giving her a kiss. "In a little while. Stay." He tossed her a treat, which she gobbled down as always.

Hunter was still standing where Nick had left him, apparently not wanting to sit. He took the water gratefully, gulping from it. Nick stayed close by in case Hunter's fingers were too shaky to hold the glass, but he seemed able to manage it.

Kneeling on the stone hearth, Nick struck a long match and held it to the twisted newspaper shoved under the waiting logs and kindling. Every morning in winter, he prepared the fireplace so it was waiting to be lit when he came home.

Then he took the empty glass from Hunter and set it on a wooden side table. Hunter's lips weren't blue, which was a good sign, and his winter gear had seemed good quality. Still, he'd been out in the growing blizzard for too long. Nick's driveway off the dirt road was a long walk in good weather, let alone snow squalls with deep drifts and that biting wind.

Knowing skin-on-skin was best for reheating, Nick rolled up his flannel sleeves and blew into his hands. "We should make sure you warm up enough. Better safe than sorry, right?"

Hunter blinked, clutching the blanket around him. "Uh…okay?"

"We'll start with the trunk and move out toward the extremities." He tried to imagine he was a doctor like Eric had been, professional and detached as he slipped his hands under the blanket and sweatshirt, wrapping them around Hunter's ribs, ignoring Hunter's little gasp and the way his blue eyes flared dark. That wasn't desire. No. It was cold, or shock.

"Oh!" Hunter laughed shakily. "You

mean… Right. Um, thank you?" He had a habit of making statements into questions.

Nodding, Nick rubbed up and around Hunter's back, warming his trembling flesh. When he swept one hand over Hunter's stomach, Hunter jolted and swayed, grabbing onto Nick's shoulder. Their eyes locked, and *shit*.

Hunter was going to be a complication in Nick's perfectly ordered life. No doubt about it.

Dropping his head, Nick concentrated on rubbing warmth back into Hunter's torso. He had to face that he'd been so angry when Hunter had called that morning because he'd been so pathetically disappointed. While he'd felled, baled, and stacked grids of spruce from one of the back acres the day before—when he should have been reveling in being alone after two solid days of people—he'd looked forward to seeing Hunter again. Looked forward to getting to know him. Teaching him.

He'd let himself be…excited.

In the eight years since Eric, Nick had fucked other guys, but few more than once, and he'd rarely been *excited* about it. And there was no guarantee Hunter even wanted to fuck him, although Nick's instincts insisted he did. Hunter intrigued him with his flashes of spirit and anxious, jittery energy. There was something about him Nick wanted to soothe. He *craved* it in a way he hadn't in a long time.

He'd planned out how he'd teach Hunter about harvesting—how he'd show him how strong he really was. When Hunter had called, Nick had felt like the biggest fool and hadn't listened. Christ, he'd actually endangered the young man's life because of his own pride. He brought his hands up over Hunter's blanketed shoulders, looking down into his wary blue eyes.

"I'm sorry," Nick said. "I should have listened to you when you called. What happened with the car?" He took hold of Hunter's arms, pushing up the cotton sleeves and rubbing, wanting to feel skin again. The fire burned steadily now, the musky smell of burning wood tangy in the warm air. Hunter had stopped shaking and chattering, and was likely just fine now, but Nick didn't drop his hands.

"Um, I hit some ice," Hunter said quietly. "I wasn't speeding, but I skidded right into the ditch. After you hung up, I lost the signal, so I couldn't call CAA. And I couldn't get the car out alone."

"I really am sorry." And he was. He squeezed Hunter's hands gently, chafing his fingers. "You're sure you weren't hurt?"

He nodded. "It was just..." Now a tremor

rippled through him. "Kind of scary."

The shame flared. "I can imagine. That wasn't an easy walk."

"I figured if I was going to die, I wanted to tell you that you were an asshole first."

There was a beat of silence aside from the crackling fire warming the air. Hunter sucked in a breath, his eyes big as he opened and closed his mouth. He looked stunned at his own words, his fingers trembling now as he added, "I—I… What I mean is…"

Instead of a burst of anger, Nick had to laugh—a loose, joyous eruption. "Honestly, more people should probably tell me that. I deserve it."

The apprehension that had darkened Hunter's face transformed into a smile that lit up his blue eyes and creased his freckled, ruddy cheeks. He laughed, a little giggle of delight and release that was utterly charming and genuine. He looked so young and intoxicatingly beautiful, his golden hair a mess from his hat.

Ella barked impatiently, and Hunter jumped, laughing nervously. "She's cute."

Nick grunted and muttered, "She's lucky she is," but he smiled at her fondly. "She thinks I'm hogging you." He whistled softly and nodded, and Ella rocketed over, practically flying, brownish ears flapping and her nails skimming over the wood floor. "Ella, this is Hunter."

Laughing, Hunter dropped to his knees on the plush blue shag rug, the blanket slipping off his shoulders to pool around him. Nick's old Banff sweatshirt hung loose on Hunter, the wide neck low over his collarbones. Nick had the absurd urge to stroke his thumb over the knobs of bone.

"Hey, girl. Nice to officially meet you." Hunter scratched behind her ears, and she licked his chin eagerly before flopping over. "You want tummy rubs, huh?"

Nick watched them, a strange sensation swelling in his chest.

That sensation is actual happiness at the company of another human, for the record. You're not having a heart attack or stroke, I assure you.

Nick smiled wryly to himself at Eric's imaginary comment.

Hunter scratched Ella's belly. "She's awesome."

"Yes. She is." She was splayed on the rug, in absolute heaven, completely innocent and guileless. Sometimes Nick loved her so much he could barely stand it.

He cleared his throat. "Did you want to use the land line to call anyone?"

"Oh. Right." Hunter withdrew from Ella

almost guiltily and stood. Ella rubbed against his calves. "Um, I'll call CAA and get out of your hair? Unless you wanted to do some work?" He glanced at the window.

Nick squinted at the swirl of white. "Not happening today." He frowned. "And I'm not throwing you out. I just thought your mother might be worried."

Hunter sucked in a breath. "Shit, she probably is. That would be awesome if I can call."

"Of course."

It occurred to Nick that it was time for breakfast, his stomach growling. He usually only drank black coffee in the mornings before returning from the trees for a hearty brunch.

He asked Hunter, "Are you hungry?"

Hunter's face lit up, and *goddamn*, he was pretty. "Starving."

"Bacon and eggs sound good?"

"Definitely. Are you sure… It's just that—" He shook his head. "I might have inhaled a little carbon monoxide, so maybe this is all some fever dream since you're being weirdly nice now? I'm probably actually unconscious and near death in my car knowing my luck."

Nick had to laugh—and once again, it felt *good*. "This is real, I assure you." Hunter's joke registered with a tug of concern. "Are you serious about the carbon monoxide?"

"Yeah, I had the engine on for a couple of minutes and the tailpipe was definitely blocked, but then I realized and got out of the car fast."

"Good boy."

He'd said it without thinking, the words flowing naturally. Nick was about to apologize in case it came across as condescending, which truly hadn't been his intent. But the words died as he watched the way Hunter's breath caught, his body rippling, tongue darting out to lick his lips.

Oh yes, look at that, Eric murmured in Nick's mind. *He likes it. He wants to be a good boy for you.*

Nick had felt horribly guilty about wanting sex after the fog of grief had slowly lifted in the first few years after Eric's death. But over time the Eric in his mind had encouraged him. While the grief would never fully leave him, it had ebbed and flowed and transformed as the years passed.

Before he knew what he was doing, Nick stepped close to Hunter, who watched him like a deer in headlights. Nick said, "It's been hours, so I'm sure you're fine. But let me take a closer look to check that your pupils aren't dilated."

"Oh. Okay." Hunter stared up at him as Nick leaned in.

The pupils in his lake-blue eyes looked

normal, or at least not massive the way they would if something was amiss. The wind-burned red on Hunter's face had faded, and the pink tinge to his skin looked like healthy warmth now—or arousal and embarrassment, not carbon monoxide.

"Looks normal." Nick tried to think of the other symptoms. "You haven't been dizzy or drowsy? Sick to your stomach?"

Hunter shook his head, still staring up at Nick. Their bodies were only a few inches apart, and it wasn't simply heat from the fireplace Nick felt coursing through him. He blurted, "Lips."

Adam's apple bobbing, Hunter rasped, "What?" Then he licked said lips, making them glisten again.

Nick managed a smile. "Cherry red lips. That's another sign." His gaze dropped to Hunter's mouth, and he clenched his fingers to resist the urge to touch. "Yours are more pink. I think you're safe." He forced his eyes back up to Hunter's, his skin prickling at the clear desire shining from those blue depths.

"Okay." Hunter nodded. "Thank you. I think I'm good. Unless my dying brain is just being generous by letting me enjoy this fantasy."

A spark of anticipation flickered through Nick. "Fantasy?"

The blush in Hunter's cheeks darkened now, and he fidgeted, trying to laugh, his gaze dropping. "Oh! Just, you know. Um, being warm?" He motioned to the fire before dropping to the rug to pet Ella again, much to Ella's slobbery delight. Hunter still didn't look up at Nick as he added, "And having a sweet dog to pet. Also bacon. Bacon is amazing."

"It is," Nick agreed, trying not to smile.

Oh yes, this pretty boy wants you. No doubt about it. What a shame you're trapped here together in such terrible weather with nothing else to do...

Nick could imagine the light in Eric's brown eyes and his mischievous laughter. Nick's own smile faded, one of the other things Hunter had said nagging. "I really am sorry about earlier, and if I wasn't overly friendly to you at the mall. I don't..." He exhaled noisily. "I'm generally not great with people, but I don't want it to be 'weird' if I'm nice."

Hunter did look up then, his eyes widening. "Oh, I didn't mean—"

"No, don't apologize. I was an asshole, as you said." He impulsively added, "Will you let me make it up to you?"

"Um, well..." Hunter took a shallow breath, his voice going hoarse, his hand frozen on Ella's back. "How?"

The possibilities were endless, and images of

Hunter naked and writhing under Nick's hands and tongue flashed through his mind. He was able to keep his tone light. "I'll start with bacon. Go ahead and use the phone to call whoever you like."

He escaped to the kitchen, his socked feet sliding a bit on the wood. He put the cast-iron pan on the range before turning on the gas, the flame making a satisfying *whoomp*. From the corner of his eye, he watched Hunter unzip his cell phone from his jacket pocket, Ella at his heels.

Nick couldn't help but listen as Hunter returned to the couch and called someone from the old phone on the side table. He was talking to CAA from the sounds of it.

"*Tomorrow*? Wow. Okay, yeah. Do I have to call back, or… Uh-huh. Yeah, I'm pretty sure I know where it is on the road."

Hunter spoke more, giving directions. Nick found himself smiling over the sizzling bacon, Ella eagerly rubbing against his legs, the lure of food drawing her into the kitchen.

Clearly Hunter should stay the night. It would be a foolish, unnecessary risk for Nick to attempt to drive him back to Pinevale in his pickup, and if the roads were closed it was pointless.

Hunter would just have to stay. It was as simple as that.

Chapter Five

O F COURSE HUNTER staying the night was a *terrible* idea, but Nick couldn't seem to do anything but grin to himself as Hunter hung up with CAA.

"I assume you got all that? They are way over capacity. Said they'll come tomorrow and tow the car back to my mom's house, or a garage if it's damaged. So…"

Nick took the carton of eggs out of the fridge, glancing over to see Hunter watching him with apprehension and an unmistakable flicker of eagerness. Nick said, "So you should stay the night. I have a guest room. You'll be safe here."

Hunter bit his lip. "You really don't mind? I don't want to be a pain." Nick could almost see the insecurity and self-doubt flood Hunter's mind. "I'm sure I can figure something out.

Maybe I can—"

"You can stay." He repeated, "You'll be safe here. And welcome. All right?"

"Yeah? Okay, cool."

"How do you like your eggs?"

"Huh? Oh! Uh, over-easy?"

"Is that how you like them? You don't sound sure."

"Yes." He laughed nervously. "Over-easy, please."

"Done." Nick returned to the pan and grabbed the bacon with tongs, plopping the strips on a paper-towel-covered plate while shooing Ella away.

He realized with a pang that Hunter would be the first man to sleep over since Eric's death. A few had come over for sex, but Nick had never considered having them stay. Granted, there was a raging blizzard, and he couldn't exactly turn Hunter out.

Of course he heard Eric's teasing brogue in his mind on cue.

You want him to stay, and the blizzard is very convenient, isn't it? He's a beautiful boy. Why shouldn't he stay? You've been a lonely grump far too long, my love.

Nick couldn't argue that he'd been alone a long time. He hadn't thought of himself as particularly lonely, but... Regardless, he shouldn't get ahead of himself.

John had said Hunter lived in Toronto, and this would obviously only be a holiday fling—assuming *it* even happened. Hunter might end up sleeping in the guest room after all. He was staying a night—not moving in.

Hunter's voice came from the couch as Nick cracked the eggs into the greasy pan. "Hey, Mom. Yeah, it's crazy, huh? Is it bad in town?" He was silent a few moments, then he said, "Wow. Way more snow than they were calling for. It's a blizzard out here. And I'm fine, but—" He sighed heavily. "*Mom.* I just said I'm fine. Would you let me finish? The car slid into a ditch, but I'm not hurt. I don't think there's any damage to the car, but I'm not positive. CAA said they'll get it tomorrow and tow it to you." After a pause, he said, "I'm not hurt at all, I promise. Yeah, I'm going to stay the night. Uh-huh. He's really nice."

Nick gave him a dubious smirk as he grabbed the sourdough loaf from atop the fridge. Hunter said into the phone, "Okay. Love you too, Mom. Walk carefully tomorrow." He hung up.

"'Really nice' is a generous assessment," Nick noted.

Hunter shrugged. "It's like with the kids. You were actually sweet with them in the end."

"Hmm." He flipped the eggs. "Am I being

sweet with you now?" He hadn't meant it to sound suggestive, but somehow it had.

Hunter shifted on the couch, looking a little flustered. "I dunno. I guess?"

Guilt still nagged. "You really could have ended up in a bad way this morning. I didn't realize a storm was blowing in."

"It's okay, really."

Nick put two slices of bread in the toaster. "I don't know if I deserve your forgiveness."

"Well, you have it." There was no question in Hunter's tone, and when Nick glanced over, Hunter nodded seriously. "Don't worry about it anymore. I'm fine, and you're making it up to me, remember?"

Their gazes held, silence in the house but for the fire crackling and eggs sizzling. Nick nodded slowly. "I will." *Oh,* he was going to make it up to Hunter all right. He was going to—

The toast popped up, and they both jerked before laughing. Nick quickly slid the eggs from the pan onto plates before they overcooked, and put down two more pieces of bread in the toaster.

"Can you grab a couple place mats and cutlery? In those two drawers." He nodded toward them. "We can eat by the window." His round dining table of sturdy oak and four matching chairs sat by the wide expanse of glass.

Feet silent in the big socks Nick gave him, Hunter padded over to the kitchen. He gave Ella—clearly torn between him and staying near the bacon—more rubs and set the table, humming a carol. "Joy to the World," Nick thought. He rarely heard Christmas music nowadays—although he'd gotten his fill at the mall—but he found he liked Hunter's gentle hum.

Nick fetched the butter crock and brought their plates and toast to the table, putting the plates on the cork-backed place mats, which depicted forest and lake scenes painted by the Group of Seven.

After tossing Ella a piece of bacon, he pointed to her bed and snapped his fingers. She went, gobbling down the meat. She'd be giving them puppy eyes, but Nick didn't let her beg by the table. If she was good, she'd get another bacon strip when they were finished.

As Hunter sat, he seemed to realize he was humming and broke off with a guilty expression. "Sorry. I can't get Christmas music out of my head."

Nick smiled. "Peril of the job. Orange juice? Or I can put more coffee on. I don't have any tea." Being a Scot, Eric had drank it daily, but Nick had never taken to it.

"Juice is awesome, thanks." Hunter slathered butter on his toast and dipped it into an egg, smearing the yolk around. "Mmm. This is perfect."

Nick got their juice and sat across from him at the round table. They ate in comfortable quiet, the wind howling, trees barely visible through the whiteout. The fire roared, keeping them toasty while Mother Nature raged, and the meal was salty and hearty. It really was perfect. Nick couldn't recall the last time he'd felt so...*peaceful* in someone's company.

Eventually, Nick said, "John mentioned you came out in high school. Impressive."

Hunter shrugged, swiping with his tongue at a dribble of yolk in the corner of his mouth. "My one moment of bravery. I got so pissed with the teasing I couldn't take it anymore. My friend Shelby thinks the bully was probably in the closet. Maybe she's right."

"That's often the way it seems to go. And I'm sure there's much more bravery in you. Don't sell yourself short."

Hunter scoffed. "I doubt it."

Ignoring that, Nick asked, "Then you went to U of T?" He took a bite of warm, buttery bread.

"Yeah, for the all the good it did me. If you want to know about the arbitrary nature of rule itself in Arthurian legend, I can tell you all about it. Not much good in the real world. But

I always sucked at math and science—my brain just doesn't work that way, you know? So I got my English degree, and now… I don't know. I figured marketing and communications since I'm a pretty good writer. I've had three unpaid internships—doing mostly promo type of stuff. There don't seem to be any actual jobs. It's a little depressing."

Nick remembered his judgment of Hunter wanting to be paid for being an elf and felt like an ass. "That's frustrating. Although I don't think education is ever useless. I never went to university, and I wish I had sometimes."

"Yeah, I guess. I just feel like…" He toyed with a strip of bacon, picking it up and shredding off a piece. "I should be getting a real job, like in an office. But I don't think I really want to. I mean, I know most people don't like their jobs, but the whole nine-to-five thing in the city? My soul was being sucked out already. But obviously I need to suck it up."

"And be miserable?" Hunter's uncertainty and turmoil made Nick want to reach for him. He kept hold of his cutlery. "Don't make yourself unhappy doing something you believe you 'should.' There are plenty of things people think *I* should do. But I know myself."

"Yeah, I mean, you're so…" Hunter waved his hand. "Confident and stuff." He chewed the bacon and asked, "Do you enjoy your job?"

"I do, yes. Always have."

"What's it like? I know you cut down the trees to sell in November and December, but what about the rest of the year?"

"January and February are quiet. I still check on the trees regularly, so I keep busy. Spring is planting season, of course. Have to watch the late frosts here. Then the warmer months are filled with weeding and insect-management. Also shearing to make sure the trees grow in the right shape."

Hunter frowned. "What do you mean?"

"Douglas firs are generally a natural cone shape that people want for Christmas trees, but I still have to keep an eye on them. Scotch pine needs regular shearing, though."

"Huh. I guess I thought Christmas trees just…grew like that."

"Not in the perfect shape, I'm afraid. My job would be a lot easier if I didn't have to shear and guide them."

"How many trees do you have?"

"About seventy-five thousand on fifty acres."

Hunter's eyebrows shot up. "Whoa. That sounds like a lot."

"It's big enough. There are massive operations that would dwarf my farm, and smaller ones as well. It's a lot of work for one person, but I manage. I'm used to long days."

Eric's voice piped up with: *Yes, because if you're a workaholic, you don't have time to think about how lonely you've become out here.*

"Wow." Hunter scratched at his neck, and Nick's eyes dropped to his collarbones before he forced his gaze back to his plate. "Do people come and cut their own trees?"

"Hell no." Nick grimaced at the thought. "I sell to nurseries and stores. Last thing I want is people tramping around here with axes they don't know how to use."

Hunter chuckled. "Fair enough. I remember going to some place when I was a kid, and we made a wreath."

"Mmm. I sell greenery for that. Wreaths are good business. Does your mom do a tree?"

"Um…" Hunter winced.

Nick had to laugh. "Don't tell me she has a fake tree. You know those things will sit in a landfill forever."

"I know! If it's any consolation, it's the same old tree we've had as long as I can remember." He peered around. "For a Christmas tree farm, there is a distinct lack of holiday decoration."

Nick hadn't really thought about it. "I suppose there is. Doesn't seem worth it when it's just me and Ella. She'll probably try to eat everything anyway." He thought back to something Hunter had said earlier. "Where's your mom walking to tomorrow? You mentioned it on the phone. Sorry for eavesdropping."

"It's okay—hard not to hear when we're in the same room. She works at the hospital, and it's close enough to walk since she won't have the car back."

"Ah." Distant memories of Eric and that gray brick building flitted through his mind. "What's her name? John mentioned it, but I can't recall."

"Pam Adams?"

"Hmm. I don't know if I ever met her." He realized Hunter might not understand what he was talking about, but before he could explain, Hunter nodded.

"I think once or twice? She remembered you. And…him, obviously." Hunter glanced toward the fireplace. "Is that… Is he with you in that picture?"

The rustic wooden mantel was an old railway tie, and there were a few framed pictures atop it. "Yes. Eric." Nick looked toward the photos across the room even though he'd seen them a million times. "That was on my birthday one year. Long time ago now."

The memory was faded, a summer barbecue at the cottage of a friend Nick hadn't spoken to in years. He'd drifted away from almost everyone, and if not for John's stubbornness, he wouldn't know any of the old group anymore.

"He had a great smile."

Nick smiled himself, bittersweet memories filling his mind before receding. "He did. He was brilliant, although he struggled to believe that sometimes. His parents were harsh." They hadn't approved of his homosexuality either, and Nick was glad they were back in Scotland and he'd never had to deal with them.

"What about your parents?"

"I never knew my father. My mother died years ago now." The distant ache of her loss was familiar and bittersweet in its own way. "Lost touch with the rest of the family over the years. My brother lives in BC. We email once in a while."

Hunter was quiet a moment. "I didn't know my father either. It sucked, but it was what it was. My mom's amazing, and so's my sister."

Nick went to the fireplace and tossed in a couple logs, sparks spraying. He nodded to the mantel and the other silver-framed pictures. "The golden retriever's Max, and that's John and Desmond with me and Eric in that one shot."

"I've never actually met Desmond, but I'm sure he's great. John's always been awesome to me."

"They're good friends. Stubborn friends,

luckily for me." From her bed in the kitchen, Ella whined. Nick laughed. "Want to give her that last piece of bacon? Unless you want it."

"I could never deprive her." Hunter went and knelt by her bed, and she licked his face while he laughed, the sweet, low sound echoing through the house. He stood and grabbed the bacon, Ella practically leaping up to the counter.

Nick should have scolded her, but he didn't as Hunter fed her, still laughing. Instead, Nick said, "She lives to eat."

The phone rang, and Ella barked. Nick shushed her as he went to pick up the receiver by the couch. He still had an old wired phone since cordless receivers didn't work in power outages, and in an ice storm electricity could go out for days. "Hello?"

John's deep, cheerful voice filled his ear. "Nick! How's it going out there? Thought I'd check in on you."

"We're fine. Getting a lot more snow than expected but still have power. Can't complain."

"We, huh? Wasn't sure if Hunter would make it. How's he working out?"

"We can't do much until the storm passes, but..." He cleared his throat. "I'm sure he'll be a hard worker. For now we're snowed in."

John's laughter boomed. "You're fucking him already, aren't you?"

"What? No!"

"Oh, don't try to deny it. I know you too well, my friend. If you haven't tapped that fine ass yet, you will soon."

Nick grumbled, "Whatever."

"Well, that works out for me, because I have another favor to ask."

"No. Whatever it is, no."

"There's one more weekend of Santa's Village. There's buzz around town about hot Santa. You're such a recluse, and people are curious. And if you and Hunter are fucking, I'm sure you won't mind spending more time ogling him in his tights."

He wanted to deny the ogling, but couldn't with Hunter listening—and because it would be a lie. "I have too much work."

"May I remind you that it's for charity? Think of the children."

"You're a son of a bitch, you know that?"

"Yep. You and Hunter enjoy yourselves. See you Saturday!"

"Yeah, yeah." Nick hung up and turned back to Hunter. "Well, I guess we'll be teaming up in Santa's Village again this weekend."

Hunter grinned. "I guess John really can get you to do something you don't want to."

Nick chuckled. "Yes. One of the few." He smiled over at Ella. "And her, of course."

Hunter toyed with the frayed seam on one

of the sweatshirt's cuffs. "I guess we really are snowed in, huh?"

"Seems that way." Anticipation skipped through him as Hunter neared to stand before him on the blue rug.

Hunter asked, "What should we do?" He peeked up at Nick through his thick lashes. Was he trying to be…seductive? Nick honestly couldn't tell, but he hoped so.

Of course the best thing to do would be to put physical distance between them. Stay professional. Avoid complications.

Eric's voice echoed again before Nick banished it.

Oh, however will you pass the time? The poor lad still needs warming up, surely…

Nick heard himself say, "I promised I'd make it up to you. Being such an ass earlier."

Hunter stared up at him, his lips parting. He scratched his neck, tugging down the low collar of the baggy sweatshirt. Before Nick could shove his hands in his pockets, he was reaching out and brushing his thumb over the knob of a collarbone. Hunter sucked in a little gasp.

Nick pulled his hand back. "I'm sorry. I shouldn't have done that. That was inapprop—"

Hunter lunged, kissing him forcefully, his arms looping around Nick's neck and tugging him down. He'd apparently found another moment of bravery inside him, and Nick felt strangely proud of him.

The kiss was clumsy—but, *oh*, the hunger in it fired Nick's blood. He opened his mouth, urging Hunter's lips to part so their tongues could meet.

The sweatshirt bunched up under his hands, and Nick stroked Hunter's back, stopping at the cotton of his underwear even though he wanted to rip them off, the PJ bottoms sliding low on Hunter's hips. Ella barked, butting against their legs.

Moaning as he gasped into Nick's mouth, Hunter rubbed against him, actual static electricity sparking on the flannel of Nick's shirt. Hunter yelped and jerked back, laughing. Nick smiled, and they both laughed at Ella by their feet, barking and confused by what exactly her master was doing.

Nick snapped his fingers and ordered her back to the kitchen. "Bed. Now." She hesitated, barking softly and looking between Nick and Hunter. Then she obeyed, still tense and giving them a decidedly judgy glare.

Laughing softly, Hunter ran his palms over Nick's pecs with awe. "Oh my God, did I really do that? Is this really happening?"

Nick held Hunter's waist. "Do you want this to happen?"

"Yes." He nodded vigorously, meeting

Nick's eyes.

"You're feeling all right?"

"Uh-huh," Hunter breathed, his arms snaking around Nick's waist as he thrust his swelling cock against Nick's hip. "I could have died out there, and I don't really know what I'm doing, but I'm positive I want to do this. I need…" He panted softly, licking his lips. "I need to get out of my own way." He stared up at Nick, his expression open and vulnerable. "Will you help me? Please?"

Nick slid a hand beneath the sweatshirt, teasing one of Hunter's nipples. Hunter shivered as Nick circled rhythmically with his thumb. "You need to get out of your own way?"

Tensing, Hunter dropped his gaze. "That must sound stupid. It's something my friend Shelby says, and—never mind."

There it was, that anxious self-doubt that Nick instinctively wanted to calm. He could practically hear Hunter berating himself, and he wanted to take control and give him the freedom to stop worrying. To help ground him. He pressed his palm over Hunter's thudding heart.

Hunter was still doubting and tense. "I need… I don't know what. I'm such a mess."

"Maybe you need a daddy." As Nick said it, it felt *right,* and goddamn, he wanted this.

More than he'd thought.

Hunter stared up at him, his eyes widening as he whispered, "What?" He looked truly shocked, his hands jerking on Nick's waist before dropping, his fingers twisting anxiously.

Damn it. Nick had gone too far. "Never mind." He stepped away, though his body protested, his cock demanding friction and his hands eager for more skin. "I need to..." He cast about for tasks. "Stoke the fire and let Ella out."

But Hunter reached for him, snagging Nick by his belt. "Wait." He looked down at his hand, as if surprised to see it grabbing onto the black leather. Brow creasing, he licked his lips. "Did you mean..."

"It was inappropriate. You're probably still in shock from the accident." This was the part when Nick would gently ease Hunter's fingers from his belt and walk away.

Any second now.

Hunter stepped closer, the rug thick beneath their feet. Nick gripped with his toes in his wool socks instead of walking away like he was supposed to.

Yep. Any second now. Walking away. He'd gone too far.

"So you *did* mean like..." Hunter blinked up at him. "Like *that?*"

Lust hung thick in the air with the husk of

their breathing and a spray of sparks in the fireplace as a log shifted. Nick couldn't look away from Hunter's hopeful blue eyes, glowing with such innocence and desire.

Then Hunter dropped his hand and head, shoulders hunching. He crossed his arms like a shield. "Never mind. I'm an idiot. The cold obviously affected my brain. I shouldn't have kissed you."

Sighing in silent relief, Nick took Ella outside, cooled off, and he and Hunter spent the rest of the day with polite distance between them as they watched movies. The next day, Hunter went home, and Nick returned to his solitude, so busy with work he barely had time to think of anything, let alone the narrow escape he'd made from an enticing complication he didn't need in his life.

Well.

That would have been the smart thing to do, but Nick couldn't bear the defeat in Hunter's voice—how the tremor returned as he stared at his feet, looking unbearably fragile.

So instead of walking away, Nick said clearly and confidently, "Yes. That's what I meant." When Hunter's head whipped up, his eyes wide again, Nick held his gaze and asked, "Have you ever had a daddy?"

Hunter swallowed, his Adam's apple bobbing. "No," he whispered. "But I want one."

Chapter Six

*O*H, HOW HE wanted a daddy.

Hunter could barely breathe, afraid he'd break the spell if he so much as moved an inch. He stared up at Nick, who watched him with his gray eyes hooded and intense. Unflinching.

Obviously Hunter had heard the term before—like leather daddies or whatever—but he'd never quite understood until right *now* that *this* was what he'd craved for so long. "I don't… I don't know what…" Fuck, he wanted to climb the mountain—and the man—but he didn't know how to start.

Nick stepped close, brushing a hand over Hunter's head and sending a sweet shiver down his spine. "It's all right. I'll show you."

Hunter still wasn't sure how he'd gotten the nerve to kiss Nick. Another bold impulse seized him at the intense way Nick's gaze swept down over Hunter's body with what really, really seemed like desire. The clothes were baggy, and Hunter tugged off the sweatshirt and then the PJs, not even needing to undo the drawstring since they were so big. He worked his feet out of the socks on the rug.

Now he was standing in his gray boxer briefs, breathing hard. "I know I'm too skinny, and not all buff like—"

Nick pressed a finger to Hunter's mouth. "You're beautiful." Then he bent and kissed him, and Hunter thought his heart might explode.

Ella's barking echoed, and she raced over, circling them in agitation. They broke apart, laughing. Hunter knelt on the rug and petted her. "You're a real cock-blocker, huh, girl?"

"Ella," Nick said. "Time to go out."

She leapt to obey, her tail wagging as Nick walked to the front door. A swirl of snow and arctic air blew in, and Hunter wallowed in the warmth of the fire to his right. He'd been cold as hell after his slog down Nick's incredibly long road, but now a fever sizzled through him. Being touched by those big, calloused hands was everything he'd ever dreamed of.

It was beyond surreal, kneeling there in his undies on Nick's rug. How was this actually happening? Nick had been such a dick, hanging up on him, but then he'd seemed concerned and caring, his touch so calming and strong.

I really hope I'm not actually dead and imagining all this. Although if I am, this must be freaking heaven.

Still kneeling, he watched Nick walk—no, *prowl* back to him. Nick's arms were hairy where he'd rolled up the sleeves of his plaid shirt, and with his full beard and dark, silver-sprinkled hair—not to mention his muscles—he was every inch a *man.*

I am getting out of my own way if it kills me.

Hunter's throat was dry, and he probably needed more water, but he wasn't moving. He waited, breathing shallowly, feeling the need to say something. He went with, "It's not dangerous for her to be out in this weather?"

"No, she loves the snow. She won't go far, and she can sniff her way back blindfolded. She'll play for hours in the barn watching the birds in the rafters if I let her."

"Cool. Yeah, that's...cool." *Oh God, I'm actually going to have sex.*

Nick tilted his head, watching Hunter closely. "Do you really want to do this?"

Taking a deep breath, Hunter said, "Uh-huh." The fire warmed his skin, but goosebumps still shivered over him. He tried to joke.

"It's a little late to back out now."

Nick frowned. "It's never too late to change your mind and say no."

"Oh, I know! I didn't mean…" Shit, he was screwing this up, like usual. He stood and approached Nick. "It was a stupid joke."

Not touching him yet even though Hunter was inches away, Nick nodded. "All right. If you ever want to stop for any reason, just say so."

"Right. Okay." God, it was so embarrassing that he was a virgin. Not having done anything kinky or whatever before was one thing, but was Nick really going to want to have sex with someone so clueless?

Before Hunter could say anything else, Nick leaned closer, running his rough palms down Hunter's back to the top of his ass. He whispered, his breath a hot gust, "Do you need a daddy, Hunter?"

Dick hard again in an instant, he clung to Nick's waist. "Yes." The sensation of Nick's flannel shirt against Hunter's nipples was so sexy, but he was dying to feel that hairy chest.

"Are you a good boy?"

Oh my God. Hunter was going to jizz in his underwear. "I try to be."

"Hmm. So you're a bad boy sometimes?"

Hunter rubbed against him, feeling Nick's

hardness through his work pants and wanting that cock inside him. In his mouth, his ass—Hunter didn't care. He just wanted to be owned. "I'm so bad sometimes."

"Do you need discipline?"

"Uh-huh."

Nick slapped Hunter's ass. Hard. "Good boys answer properly."

"Yes." Hunter nodded, a thrill shooting to his balls at his own words as he added, "Yes, Daddy."

With a rumbling groan, Nick kissed him, his tongue surging against Hunter's. He tasted of orange juice and pine, or maybe that was the scent filling Hunter's nose as Nick took him in his arms, almost lifting him off his feet. His kiss was commanding, and Hunter whimpered into his mouth, desire burning through him, any hint of chill eradicated.

Nick's thick beard was wonderfully rough against Hunter's face. They kissed until his head spun, his lips tingling, Nick's tongue exploring and teasing. Hunter clung to him as he gasped for air, spit stringing between their mouths. Nick ran his thumb over Hunter's lower lip, his flinty eyes dark.

"I want you naked."

Nodding, Hunter shoved down his boxer briefs and kicked them free, his cock springing up. Despite his earlier bravery, he would have agonized over whether or not to take them off, and when. It was a glorious relief to have Nick in charge.

Nick dropped his gaze over Hunter's body, and Hunter shifted, wishing he could read Nick's mind. Was he too skinny? His cock was uncut and fairly long, and he'd always thought it was a decent size? He wished he had more chest hair, though, and—

"You really are beautiful." Nick took Hunter's face in his big hands and kissed him softly. "You don't have to worry about anything. Do you trust Daddy?"

"Yes," he whispered. Maybe it was crazy since they'd just met, but he did trust Nick. He thought of him in that Santa costume and the way he'd been so kind and patient with the children. The sweet way he was with Ella and how he'd taken care of Hunter.

Nick kissed him again, and Hunter tasted a hint of the salty, wonderfully greasy bacon. Nick had actually *cooked* for him. Hunter's mom had worked such long hours, and he and Heather had often made do with sandwiches or whatever. Nick cooking for him had made him feel comforted in a way he couldn't really explain.

"You'll be safe here."

Nick's calm command eased the tension in Hunter. He gasped as Nick tweaked his nipples.

"On your knees like a good boy."

A thrill zinging through him, Hunter did as he was told. Nick towered over him, still in his work pants and plaid shirt, and it made Hunter's dick throb to be naked at his feet. He didn't know what to do with his hands, and he fidgeted with his fingers, waiting for Nick to tell him what he should do.

Nick brushed back Hunter's hair, which was probably an ugly mess after having a hat on for hours. "Hands behind your back. Don't move them until I say you can."

Hunter clasped his fingers behind him.

"Very good." Nick traced Hunter's lips before pushing his thumb inside.

Hunter circled it with his tongue and sucked, pride flushing through him when Nick's nostrils flared with desire.

"Do you want to suck Daddy's cock?"

With his lips still wrapped about Nick's thumb, Hunter nodded, moaning. *God,* how he wanted to suck that cock. Nick pulled his thumb free and unbuckled his belt. He eased the leather free of its loops, dropping the belt to the rug with a soft thud. As Hunter watched eagerly, still half-convinced this couldn't be real, Nick released his erection, his pants hanging open on his hips.

He was cut, flushed red, and *big*. His cock was thick, his hairy balls hanging heavy. Throat dry, Hunter waited, his fingers gripping together behind him so he didn't accidentally reach out to touch. He burned to take that meat in his mouth, bury his face in Nick's dark pubes, and give himself over to it.

But Nick didn't seem to be in any rush. Looking down at Hunter with a little smile, he unbuttoned his plaid shirt, starting at the bottom where his cock poked out. He brushed his fingers over his thick shaft, and Hunter couldn't have looked away for all the money in the world. He watched each button be loosed, his heart a drum as Nick's stomach and chest were revealed, hairy and strong and *perfect*.

Hunter didn't even realize he'd moved to take himself in hand, pleasure rippling through him until Nick barked, "No." He softened his tone as Hunter jerked his hand away from his dick. "No touching yourself unless I give you permission."

"I'm sorry, Daddy." He clasped his hands behind him again. "I didn't mean to."

"I know. That's a good boy." Sliding the plaid shirt down his back, he freed his arms and let the flannel fall to the rug. His impressive cock stood, his dark pants still on his hips. He ran his fingertip over Hunter's mouth. "Don't move. And especially don't touch yourself."

Hunter bit back a groan of frustration, watching as Nick tossed another few logs on the fire, staying out of spark range on the hearth. Then he went upstairs, and Hunter craned his neck to see, careful not to shift too much.

Nick disappeared into a bedroom at the end of the exposed hall, and Hunter held his breath, listening. The rug was soft under his knees, and he flattened his feet and sat on them.

Anticipation zipped through him. Sure, he was nervous, but it was like a puzzle piece had finally slotted into place. With Nick, kissing and touching felt right, like Hunter was made for it. He'd lusted after Nick the moment he saw him half-dressed in that Santa suit, and maybe he should have been afraid to give himself to a virtual stranger, but he wasn't.

"Maybe you need a daddy."

Balls tingling, Hunter's hard cock twitched. He clenched his hands behind him. No matter how much he wanted to jerk off, he was going to obey—and that gave him a flush of pleasure all its own. The fire roared to his right, his skin wonderfully warm.

He ached to be touched and filled, and he definitely was staying the fuck out of his own way for the first time. He wanted this. *Needed* it. And he trusted Nick to give it to him. He didn't have to worry. Nick would take care of him.

John wouldn't be friends with a serial killer, right?

He laughed under his breath. His instincts told him he was safe, and he was going to listen to them for once, refusing to let anxiety whirl up like a tornado. Staying in place, he looked around the main floor. The wide window along the side of the house was before him, the round rustic dining table and chairs sitting in the dim light. Through the glass, there was only white, and Hunter couldn't tell if it was cloudy sky as well as snow.

To the left, he peered into the kitchen. There was a big island with a couple of stools, and the cupboards were dark wood. The only thing on the counter aside from a coffeemaker and toaster was a mug. Ella's bowls were on the floor on the left side of the island, the fridge to the right. There were only a couple of magnets on the fridge, as opposed to the colorful mishmash Hunter's mom had.

Nick's house was neat and orderly, but it did look lived in. The brown leather couch looked soft, the cushions on the right side especially worn, the huge leather ottoman dipping a little on that side. Navy and dark green throw cushions were tossed aside to the left.

To his right, the massive TV over the fireplace was dark. He peered up at the thick, rustic mantel. There were no stockings hung from it yet, and it made Hunter sad to think that there wouldn't be. He'd always loved the ritual of decorating with his mom—baking sugar cookies and sipping fresh hot chocolate, listening to her jazzy holiday CDs on the old stereo.

He peered at the three framed photos on top of the mantel, going up on his knees and squinting. Eric had been handsome—short brown hair with a curl to it, a lock hanging over his forehead. He was laughing, and he looked at Nick with a glowing smile. It was awful to think of him dying in an icy lake, trying to save a doomed boy.

In the photo with Eric, Nick was smiling too, and he was younger—the silver not highlighting his dark hair yet. There was a lightness in his expression that made Hunter's heart clench. He wanted to know him. He'd never felt an attraction like this before. He wanted to know *everything*.

The floor creaked above, and Hunter jerked back into position, sitting on his heels again, not looking as Nick crossed the hall and slowly descended the stairs. His pulse raced. He wasn't sure what Nick had done up there. Had he brought something back?

As Nick stood in front of him again, Hunter stared at his huge cock, mouth dry. It had softened a bit, but was still thick and flushed, jutting out. Hunter thought about leaning forward and licking it…

"Did you touch yourself?"

Focusing, Hunter shook his head. "Not even a little."

Nick chuckled. "Good boy."

He didn't need to touch himself for another powerful wave of pleasure to roll through him. He watched as Nick eased down his pants and black briefs, stepping out of them and kicking them aside. He stood before Hunter, legs slightly spread, in all his hairy, masculine glory, like a lumberjack god from a wet dream.

"Fuck me," Hunter mumbled, not meaning to speak aloud.

Taking his cock in hand and giving it a few strokes, Nick stepped even closer. He traced Hunter's cheekbones with the shiny tip of his dick. "Later. If you're a good boy."

Hunter shuddered with lust, a thrill tingling through him all the way to his toes. "I'll be so good."

"I know." He circled Hunter's lips with the

head. "Do you want to suck this?"

"Yes." It was barely a whisper. "Can—*may* I?"

"Such good manners. You may. Keep your hands behind your back."

This is actually happening. I'm doing this.

Before his brain could have second thoughts and get in his way, Hunter opened his mouth and swallowed Nick's cock into his mouth, taking in as much as he could and sucking like his life depended on it. Nick groaned, and it was music to Hunter's ears.

He'd never blown anyone before, but he mimicked what he'd seen in porn, pulling back to lick along Nick's swelling length, tracing the bulging vein with his tongue. He was actually sucking another man's cock. He was *doing* it. Lust scorched through him.

His nostrils flared as he tried to breathe, his rhythm probably clumsy and haphazard. He licked and sucked, peeking up at Nick, who watched with lips parted, his chest rising and falling rapidly. His eyebrows were drawn near in a little frown, and he spread his hand wide over Hunter's head—not pushing or pulling, but guiding. He slowly began to thrust, fucking Hunter's mouth.

"That's it. Such a good boy for daddy."

Hunter moaned around Nick's dick, his

own leaking and so hard he was about to come without touching it at all. He wanted to choke on Nick's cock until there was nothing but the ache in his jaw and the throbbing flesh filling his mouth. He could taste the salty musk of precum, and he craved more. But it was so hard to breathe, and he coughed, pulling back, his eyes watering.

Nick caressed his head. "It's okay." He dropped to his knees, stroking down Hunter's arms, easing his hands from behind his back and holding them. Not too tightly or loosely, but securely. "When you said you didn't know what to do…" He tilted his head, watching Hunter closely. "What exactly did you mean?"

Hunter swallowed hard, squirming with embarrassment. He could feel spit dribbling from the corner of his mouth. Was he so bad at blow jobs that it was that obvious? "I've never done very much. Kissed a few times, and made out or whatever at a party. That's it." He dropped his eyes, his face hot. "I'm, like, a virgin?"

Nick made a breathy sound that was maybe a sigh, and Hunter's skin itched, acid spinning in his stomach. "I'm sorry. It's pathetic. I don't know why I haven't done it yet. I get too…knotted up, you know? In my head, I mean." He tried to laugh. "It's lame."

Nick lifted Hunter's chin with his finger

and stared into his eyes, that gray gaze so certain. "It's not lame. There's nothing wrong with taking your time."

His heart leapt. "You mean... You don't mind?"

"*Mind?*" He shook his head again, smiling softly. He leaned in and brushed their lips together, murmuring, "Baby, I don't mind at all. You're doing so well. I'm very proud of you."

Hunter's chest swelled with emotion as Nick kissed him for real now, their tongues meeting, his hands roaming down to Hunter's ass, their knees pushing together on the rug. Then Nick pushed to standing, hauling Hunter with him, almost off his feet.

He asked, "Do you want me to fuck you?"

Head light, Hunter nodded. "Please." He wound his arms around Nick's waist and rubbed a cheek against his bearded neck. "Please fuck me, Daddy."

Nick exhaled heavily, stroking down over Hunter's ass and squeezing. "You need my cock, hmm?"

"*Yes.*" He vibrated with need, eager and nervous all at once, but not going back.

Nick kissed him deeply, sucking on his tongue, and Hunter wondered if he could taste his own cock. Then Nick spread the forgotten blanket on the couch and sat in the middle, urging Hunter to straddle his powerful legs. Hair tickled Hunter's inner thighs, and he rocked, spreading his fingers over Nick's chest, raking his nails through the coarse fur there.

There was a bottle of lube on the couch cushion beside them, along with a foil-wrapped condom. After slicking his fingers, Nick reached behind Hunter and circled his hole, the pad of one finger teasing. He watched Hunter closely as he pushed the finger barely inside.

"Do you ever do this to yourself?"

Panting already, Hunter nodded. "Sometimes." With his knees on the couch next to Nick's hips, he gained leverage and rose up a few inches so he could push down on Nick's finger.

"So naughty," Nick murmured with a smile, pressing another slick finger inside without warning.

Hunter gasped, tensing before lowering down again, loving the burn as Nick's fingers penetrated him. "*Oh,*" he murmured. It had never felt like this when he'd fingered himself. The angle was so much better, his ass stretching open. Their cocks were hard, butting against each other with teases of friction.

"You're going to be so tight around my cock. Going to make Daddy come so hard."

Flushed with pride, Hunter squeezed his ass, ignoring the pain. "Yes."

With his other hand, Nick teased Hunter's nipples, pinching and rolling them until they stung wonderfully, oversensitive and rigid. He continued stretching Hunter's ass, the sensations rippling through Hunter until all he could do was moan.

Finally, Nick withdrew his fingers, and Hunter whimpered at the loss. Nick kissed him long and slow and wet. "Don't worry, baby. You're going to be so full you'll think you might break. But you won't, I promise. I'm here. I'll take care of you."

He urged Hunter up higher on his knees, and Hunter clung to Nick's shoulders as Nick rolled on the condom and slicked it with more lube. "Here you go. Take my cock like I know you can."

Hunter sank down, fumbling to get the head lined up with his hole. Running his palm over Hunter's back, Nick murmured, "Slow and steady. Don't hurt yourself." He quirked a dark eyebrow. "Trust me, I'm not going anywhere." He helped nudge his cock against the opening of Hunter's ass.

With a shaky laugh, Hunter tried to relax against the intrusion. "You're so big," he blurted, the burn intense.

"You can do it. I know you can." He watched Hunter with such confidence.

Hunter took a deep breath and blew it out,

screwing his eyes shut and hanging onto Nick's shoulders as he bore down. His thighs trembled, the stretch bringing tears to his eyes as he impaled himself on Nick's cock. Then it was like something gave, and he groaned as he sank all the way, letting gravity help.

"Look at me."

In a daze, Hunter obeyed, opening his eyes. Nick stroked his spine gently. "Good boy. You feel incredible." He reached down to run his fingers around the rim of Hunter's stretched ass where they were joined. "How does it feel to have me inside you?"

"Full." Hunter laughed, shaking his head. "I can't believe this is happening. I didn't expect this when I woke up this morning."

Nick's chest rumbled with laughter. "Me either. Yet here we are." He caught Hunter's mouth in a kiss, then whispered against his lips, his beard tickling. "You're beautiful." He took hold of Hunter's hips and thrust up. "So sweet and tight for Daddy."

Hunter could only cry out as Nick speared him again. He let himself relax—well, as much as he could with a massive cock splitting him open—giving himself over and letting go. He started to lift and lower, finding Nick's cadence. That wonderful cock stretched and filled him deeper than he'd thought possible.

Pleasure obliterated the pain, and Hunter's

cock strained, desperate for friction. But he kept his hands digging into Nick's broad shoulders since Nick had told him not to touch himself. He realized the cries and moans filling the air were his, and a pulse of embarrassment at how shameless he sounded squirmed through him. He snapped his mouth shut.

"No." Nick dug his fingers into Hunter's hips. "Let me hear you. You're a slut for my cock, aren't you? *Aren't you?*"

"Yes!" Hunter admitted, releasing another high cry as pressure hit his prostate just right.

"Don't be ashamed. You're gorgeous." Nick thrust up harder now, pulling Hunter down in a rough rhythm. "Made for this. Made for my cock."

Sweat glistened on Nick's forehead and in the hollow of his throat, and Hunter leaned down to lick it, the salt tangy on his tongue. Sweat gathered on his own skin, the heat from the fire on his back—heat *everywhere*. He was going to explode with it, his muscles shaking as he pleaded, "Please."

"You want to come, baby?"

"Yes," he croaked. "Need to."

"Do you think you've been well-behaved enough for Daddy to let you come?"

Hunter nodded so hard his jaw clacked together. With a smile, Nick wrapped his hand around Hunter's dick, twisting and tugging.

"Come like a good boy."

After only three strokes, Hunter did, spraying Nick's chest with jizz. Seeing the white globs land there on the dark hair made Hunter come even harder, and he squeezed convulsively on Nick's iron cock inside him as he shot again, his cries echoing in the rafters.

He clung to Nick, panting as Nick fucked up into him, groaning as he came as well. Hunter wished there was no condom and that he could feel the wetness of cum inside him.

The tension finally released, and Hunter slumped, Nick holding him close and caressing his fevered skin, murmuring, "Such a good boy."

Panting softly against his neck, Hunter kissed him. "Thank you, Daddy."

Mall Santas weren't supposed to be hot, and they also weren't supposed to be sexy lumberjacks who fucked you within an inch of your life and made you crave more. It seemed like days ago that Hunter had been stuck in the ditch and freezing his ass off trudging through the blizzard. Now he was safe and warm, and freaking *finally* no longer a virgin. Nick's softening cock was still inside him, and it was amazing.

He'd never considered whether Christmas miracles were real, but Hunter decided he was definitely a believer.

Chapter Seven

ELLA WASN'T QUITE barking or growling, but pacing at the bottom of the stairs and making a low noise of discontent—followed by a full-on whine. Nick ignored his urge to go back down and give her another kiss and treat as he and Hunter approached the bedroom door just before nine p.m.

"Aww," Hunter said. "She doesn't want to be left behind."

"She knows she's not allowed upstairs. It's only because you're here, and you're her new favorite person in the world since you've been indulging her all day with belly rubs."

Hunter seemed pleased by that, a bright smile on his face. "I'll miss you too, girl," he called. "I'll see you in the morning." The sweatshirt hung off him, and he'd rolled the sleeves up over his wrists. One had slipped down now, and he toyed with the cuff, glancing at Nick nervously.

A *virgin.*

Nick would never have guessed it given how gorgeous Hunter was, and that he was out of university. How had he not had sex before today? He'd begged so prettily, and Nick had wanted to ease him through it—make it as good as possible for a first time. He was confident he'd succeeded, and for his part, he'd had the most powerful orgasm he could remember in a long time.

"Let me just give her one more minute." Hunter hurried back down the stairs, tugging up the too-big PJs, Ella yelping with joy and licking his face as he knelt to pet her, laughing as she slobbered on him. Nick watched with a smile.

He and Hunter had spent the rest of the day watching movies, and Nick had to admit they'd...*cuddled,* Ella heavy on their laps on the couch being spoiled rotten, the fire crackling and mindless gun battles on TV.

It had been the most relaxing day Nick could remember in ages. There had been no more daddy/boy talk—he preferred to keep that roleplaying for sex and not have it bleed into everyday life. Some people enjoyed a twenty-four-seven dom/sub dynamic, but Nick liked a more equal balance.

Not that he and Hunter would have a routine or *life* together or anything even close. Christ, they'd barely met—it was still day one. This would be a temporary diversion. Hunter might not even want to have sex again—although Nick really hoped he did. Nick hadn't initiated anything else, and although they'd sat close on the couch, Hunter snug under his arm, they'd only kissed briefly.

On the threshold of his bedroom, it struck Nick again that Hunter was the first man to spend the night since Eric's death. He hesitated for a heartbeat as Hunter's footsteps thudded softly back up the stairs toward him, then he pushed the door open all the way and switched on the overhead light.

He'd fucked other men in the bed—which was a new one he'd bought a few years prior. It was beyond foolish to make a big deal of the fact Hunter would be sleeping there.

"It's nice," Hunter said, following tentatively and peering around. He shut the door, chuckling as Ella's indignant bark of protest echoed.

"Thanks. It's comfortable." Nick looked around at the king-sized bed in a rustic wooden frame to the right, matching side tables with dark orange glass lamps, a tall dresser, and multicolored throw rugs on either side of the bed.

Hunter motioned to the framed artwork—Group of Seven prints of windswept trees. "Those are pretty." He approached the window opposite the door and pulled aside a dark curtain. "Oh, there's a river! I think." He cupped his hands around his eyes. "Not much moon tonight with the clouds, but at least the snow has stopped blowing."

Nick flipped off the light so they could see better before joining him, their arms brushing. He burned to pull Hunter close and touch him all over, but since Hunter couldn't just leave, Nick refused to make him feel obligated. "Yes, it's a small river. Cuts through this corner of the property."

"Do you skate on it?"

Nick hadn't skated in years, and never on this particular river, but the thought of anyone out on the ice gripped him with a pulse of fear that sucked the air from his lungs.

He managed, "No," and sounded normal enough that Hunter didn't seem to notice anything amiss, still peering out the glass at the faint curve of the river hugging the clearing, dark forest beyond.

"It's beautiful. I can't wait to see the trees." He looked up at Nick. "Assuming you still want my help."

"Yes." He was relieved to be back on solid ground, shoving away thoughts of icy water. "I'll teach you to use the baler. There's a lot of work to catch up on." He was looking forward to it, and undeniably glad Hunter wouldn't be vanishing come morning.

"Is it cool if I shower before bed?" Hunter asked. "I usually do."

"Of course. I'll get you towels. The bathroom's in there." He nodded toward the en suite, turning on the overhead light before grabbing towels from the linen closet in the hall. He ignored Ella's huffs before shutting the bedroom door again.

"Whoa," Hunter said when Nick joined him in the bathroom. "That's a hell of a shower."

"I suppose it is," Nick agreed with a smile.

The tile was slate gray, the spacious shower extending across the rear of the bathroom with multiple jets embedded in the walls and overhead. Double sinks in an off-white vanity with a wide mirror were to the right, the toilet to the left.

Christ, Nick wanted to tug Hunter under the jets and kiss him until they couldn't breathe, but... Although Hunter had begged to be fucked—and it had been incredible—it had all moved so fast, and the responsible thing was to put on the brakes.

"Enjoy it," Nick said, passing over the towels.

"Um, yeah. Thanks?"

Nick nodded and closed the door behind him, giving Hunter privacy. He stood by the window and heard the water turn on after a minute.

A *virgin.*

Nick hadn't been with a virgin in… Jesus, possibly decades. On one hand he felt incredibly old, but it also filled him with a tenderness he hadn't experienced in a very long time.

He'd been telling the truth when he'd said he didn't mind that Hunter was a virgin. How could he *mind* that Hunter had been so eager to gift Nick his body, being his good boy with such pure passion?

After the sex, Hunter had been warm and pliant in his arms, pressing wet little kisses to Nick's neck and nuzzling against his beard. Nick would have been content to stay there for hours, but he'd cleaned them up, and they'd gotten dressed. He'd wanted to give Hunter time to process what they'd shared.

Now they were going to sleep together, and Nick felt strangely out of his depth.

A *virgin.*

Had he been considerate enough? Did Hunter want to have sex again? He had to leave the ball in Hunter's court no matter how much he wanted to march into the bathroom, sweep him into his arms, and kiss him for hours. He had to get a grip. Fucking him was one thing. More than that was off the table. It had to be.

Why? I know I'm a hard act to follow, but you've been brooding alone in the forest for long enough.

Eric's voice stubbornly filled his head. Nick wanted to argue with it, which was surely a sign that he *had* been brooding alone too long.

He's a breath of fresh air. I like him. And you like being daddy again. Don't deny it—you were always a terrible liar.

It was true. And Hunter had so much innocent need. It called to Nick, to instincts deep within him. Eric hadn't been young and insecure the same way Hunter was, but he'd questioned himself more than he should have.

Because he'd had to be in such control at the hospital, he'd craved submission and freedom from being the one in charge. After a stressful shift, he'd come home and beg for it, wanting to be a bad boy who had to be spanked. Nick had reveled in giving him the peace and release he'd needed, finding his own soul-deep pleasure in it.

"Nick?" Hunter called.

Closing the box firmly on memories of Eric, Nick cracked the bathroom door, steam flowing around him. "Do you need something?"

"Can you come in?"

Heart leaping and cock definitely on board, Nick entered the bathroom, the air thick and humid, the mirror fogged over. Hunter had opened the glass door to the long shower stall. Christ, he truly was beautiful—his pale skin flushed, nipples starkly pink, slim muscles slick and dripping, his uncut cock half hard and oh-so tempting.

He held out a bar of soap, his lip caught between his teeth. "Can you wash my back?" He lowered his head, water-darkened hair hanging over his forehead. A little shudder rippled through him, and he looked up, squaring his shoulders. "Please, Daddy?"

It was music to Nick's ears, and he was already unbuttoning his plaid shirt as he asked, "You're sure?"

"Oh, yeah." Hunter nodded. "I'm sure."

"I don't want you to feel obligated because you're staying over."

True confusion creased Hunter's face. "I don't think that word means what you think it means."

Nick's laugh warmed his chest, lust firing

through his veins. "Well, you're the English major, so you'd know." He stripped off his clothes and joined Hunter in the shower, taking the soap and putting it back in its tray for the moment.

Because right now, he needed both hands to haul Hunter against him, Hunter going up on tiptoes and grabbing Nick's face, pushing his tongue into Nick's mouth. That little spark of independence and confidence was exactly what Nick had been yearning to see, and he let him take control of their kiss.

When they were gasping for air, Nick took the washcloth and dragged it down Hunter's back to his ass. He murmured, "Spread your legs."

Hunter eagerly did, and Nick gently probed with the cloth. "Does it hurt very much?"

"A little. About what I'd expect after having something that big up there."

Chuckling, Nick skimmed his fingers up and down Hunter's crack, the need to touch drumming through him steadily. "Did you like being fucked?"

He nodded eagerly. "I loved it."

Nick kissed him. "Such a hungry little slut, hmm?"

"Yes, Daddy."

A curl of lust simmered through him to

hear those words. Nick hadn't realized just how much he'd missed that dynamic, and Hunter had taken to it like he was born for it. Beautifully submissive but spirited and vibrant. He made Nick's blood sing—which was dangerous, since Hunter was surely going back to Toronto after the holidays, and Nick was content in his solitary life, and—

With a burst of irritation at himself, he cut off that line of thinking, giving Hunter another slow kiss. They'd just met. He should simply enjoy being together for the time being. Santa and his elf having a holiday fling, and that was all.

"I never realized—" Hunter broke off. He swallowed hard, meeting Nick's gaze. Water dripped from his nose, the hot shower spraying from above and around them. "I've always been attracted to older guys, but the whole daddy thing?" His chest rose with a sharp breath. "It turns me on so much."

"Mmm." Nick slid a hand between them, stroking Hunter's cock. "Does it make you hard to call me Daddy and be my good boy?" He could feel it did, the flesh in his grip throbbing.

"Fuck, yes." Hunter laughed before smirking. "I guess Freud would have a field day with me wanting a daddy since I grew up with a single mom."

"Probably. But I didn't have a father either, so Freud can fuck off." He ran his hands over Hunter's ass, rubbing their cocks together. "Can you feel how hard you make me when you call me Daddy?"

"Yes," Hunter breathed. "Yes, Daddy." He rubbed his cheek against Nick's before leaning back and asking, "What do you want me to do, Daddy?"

"Hmm." Nick pondered it.

"I'll do anything." His brows drew together, and Nick could practically see his mind spinning with what "anything" might entail.

"You don't have to worry about that. I'll take care of you. You don't need to worry about anything."

"Right." He exhaled, his face smoothing out. "Thank you."

Nick swept his tongue into Hunter's mouth with command. Hunter moaned, reaching up to clutch Nick's shoulders, rutting against him eagerly.

Nick wasn't sure how long they stood under the hot water, locked in an embrace as they kissed until their lips were swollen and Hunter's face had to be raw. Nick kissed his red cheek tenderly and whispered, "Let's go to bed."

Their skin was still damp, towels abandoned on the floor in the bedroom when Nick pulled back the duvet and urged Hunter onto the mattress. He left one of the orange glass lamps on low, and it was almost like firelight on Hunter's pale skin.

As much as Nick wanted to bury himself in Hunter's tight heat, he didn't want to hurt him. Instead, he said, "I'm going to eat your ass. You've been such a good boy, and you're going to come so hard with my tongue inside you."

Hunter shivered, nodding. "Yes, Daddy." He glanced around at the mattress he was kneeling on. "How should I…?"

"On your hands and knees for me. That's it. Now on your elbows. Good. Rest your cheek on the pillow." Nick crawled onto the bed behind him, barely resisting reaching out to grab the round globes of Hunter's gorgeous ass. "Now bring your arms back. That's right. Hold yourself open for me."

Hunter's fingers trembled, but he obeyed beautifully, reaching back for his ass cheeks and spreading them. "Like this, Daddy?" His cheek and shoulders rested on the bed.

"Yes. That's perfect, baby." Nick leaned in, blowing a cool stream of air, watching Hunter's hole twitch. Then he huffed warm air over it, and Hunter moaned.

With Hunter holding himself open, on display, Nick teased with a fingertip and his breath, giving him the occasional hint of his tongue—just brief, wet touches. Hunter's cock strained, and Nick eased it back toward him between Hunter's legs until he could suck the head.

Hunter cried out. "Yes! Please, Daddy. Please."

Nick swirled with his tongue, swallowing the musky, pearly drops of precum. Hunter's hands shook where he still held himself open, and when Nick let go of his cock with a wet smack, he said, "You're being such a good boy."

"I thought you were going to rim me," Hunter blurted. "Please, I need…"

Nick swallowed a chuckle and put on a stern voice. "Now you're being a bad boy. I promised I would, but you have to be patient. Or I won't let you come at all."

Hunter gasped. "No! Please. I'm sorry, Daddy. I'll be good."

"I know you will." He stroked Hunter's quivering legs, drawing soothing circles with his thumbs over the tender skin of his inner thighs. "I'll take care of you."

Hunter exhaled loudly. "Thank you."

Nick's own cock was like steel, but he had to take care of Hunter before he tended to himself. Taking pity on him—and himself—he covered Hunter's hands with his own and spread him as wide as possible before licking from his balls to the top of his ass.

Crying out, Hunter jerked. "Oh God."

He was deliciously responsive, and knowing Nick was the first man to ever taste him was like drinking fine Scotch, a smooth burn that fed Nick's hunger. He circled his tongue around Hunter's hole before finally licking into him.

As Hunter's cries of pleasure echoed off the wooden rafters, Nick ate him out, licking and kissing and nipping, burying his face in that sweet ass. He knew his beard was rough against the tender flesh, and he used it as a counter-point to the wetness of his tongue and softness of his lips.

When he reached down and fondled Hunter's balls, hair bristling his palms, Hunter seized up and came without his cock being touched. Nick licked him through it, pride swelling in his chest. Hunter was almost crying with the pleasure, and he probably would have toppled over when he was finished spurting onto the sheets if not for Nick holding him up.

Nick eased him onto his side and then his back, and Hunter looked up at him in a daze, panting through his mouth, his face red. "Oh my God," he murmured. His gaze dropped to Nick's rock-hard cock. "Can I taste you,

Daddy?"

Nick groaned, surging forward to straddle him and feed him his cock. He fucked Hunter's mouth, careful not to go too deep, knowing it wouldn't take much.

Sure enough, he came before long, gripping the headboard with one hand, petting Hunter's damp hair with the other as he spent himself, milky semen dripping out of that pretty mouth. Hunter struggled to swallow, and Nick pulled out, milking himself and letting the final drops paint Hunter's flushed cheeks.

He and Hunter were wet and messy, but Nick gathered him close and kissed him, tasting himself and whispering, "Daddy's so proud of you."

Eventually, he cleaned them up and turned out the light, Hunter smiling at him with shy, dazed pleasure. Nick curled himself around Hunter's smaller body and tried not to think about how right it felt having him in his bed.

Chapter Eight

"IS THAT YOU, sweetie?"

"Hey, Mom!" Hunter called back as he untangled his scarf from his mom's massive wreath and closed the front door, dropping his keys on the little table in the foyer. His heart thumped as she appeared in the hallway from the kitchen. "I just need to pick up my elf costume."

Be normal, he reminded himself.

Wearing purple scrubs and slippers, she came to hug him. Her hair was knotted up, which meant she was going to work soon. "I feel like I haven't seen you in weeks!" She gave him a squeeze, smelling faintly of sweet lemons.

He laughed and hugged her back. "It's only been a few days."

"Nick Spini's been working you hard, huh?" She stepped away, grinning.

Hunter knew she didn't mean anything else by it, but despite his best efforts, his face went hot, the blush spreading to the tips of his ears. He tried to sound normal. "Yeah, it's been great. Muscles I didn't even know I had are sore."

Oh yeah, terrific work on not making this sound sexual.

It was true, though—along with his wonderfully sore ass, Hunter's body ached pleasantly from the three days of manual labor. He quickly added, "I know how to use a baler now, and chop down a tree with an axe. It's really cool."

Tilting her head, a little furrow between her brows, his mom smiled. "That's great, honey."

He bent to pull off his boots. "Yeah, I never thought of myself as outdoorsy or, like, good at doing that kind of physical stuff, but it's been really satisfying."

Not making this sound less sexual, you dumbass!

His face was burning as he straightened up. "Anyway, it's been cool. How are you? How's work?"

"I'm good. Work's busy, as always." She was still watching him quizzically. "I'm glad you're enjoying spending time with Nick."

"Yeah, like I said, the work's been good.

There's so much to do."

"Mmm. There must be, since you've stayed out there four nights in a row now."

Nick had driven him home Wednesday to pack clothes and toiletries, and Hunter had told his mom it would just be easier to stay at the farm since he didn't have a car. Which was true! Sure, it also meant he could spend the nights in Nick's bed and be fucked until he was blissfully exhausted.

Hunter brushed past his mom. "Yeah, like I said, there's been a ton of work. Now I'd better hurry and get over to the mall. Nick's waiting in his truck. John convinced him to be Santa again." He laughed—too high-pitched—and escaped down the hall to his room.

He grabbed the cursed elf costume, closing his eyes for a moment and breathing deeply. The past four days had been beyond his wildest dreams. He truly did enjoy the work. They'd put in long days, and Nick was all business when they were out among the trees.

Well, *almost* all business. Butterflies flapped through Hunter's belly as he remembered how Nick had kissed him fiercely at the end of the work days when they'd climbed into the pickup truck. As soon as they were in that cab, the leather seats freezing, Nick always hauled Hunter close as if he'd been dying to touch him again. Then they fogged up the windows, Ella barking outside, demanding to be let in.

And once they'd returned to the house each day…

In the doorway of his room, Hunter closed his eyes, shivering in delight. It was like he'd been on rations before, and now he was glutting himself at an all-you-can-eat sex buffet. He grinned with a giddy thrill as he thought about Nick and how gentle and patient he was while also being dominant and perfectly demanding.

Daddy kink was *so* Hunter's thing. Lust spiked at the thought of how he'd been able to give up control and relax and be taken care of in a way that soothed…well, his *soul*.

Laughing aloud at how corny he was being, Hunter hurried back to find his mom hadn't budged, and now her hands were on her hips. Her eyebrows lifted. "You and Nick Spini?"

His heart dropped. "Huh?"

She just watched him, eyebrows still about to disappear into her hairline. There was a stray piece of tinsel caught in her hair, probably from one of the red-and-gold garlands wrapped around the bannister heading downstairs. He reached out and plucked it free, letting it drift down to the floor.

"Tinsel," he said. "Anyway, I've gotta run."

She didn't move a muscle, her gaze unwavering.

Sighing, Hunter shrugged, willing himself not to blush again and failing, heat burning his cheeks. "I guess?"

"Well. You and Nick Spini. He's a lot older than you." She watched him evenly, her voice calm as she crossed her arms. She didn't seem mad, which was good. Although sometimes she would go horribly quiet when she was really furious.

"Yeah. It's cool, though. I..." He shrugged again. "I really like him."

"Mmm." She still stared like she could see right into his mind in that way moms had. "He's been good to you?"

"Yes," he answered without hesitation. "He's great. I thought he was a jerk at first, but he's not at all." Hunter tried to find the right words. "He's so..."

His mom laughed softly, shaking her head. "Dreamy? You should see the expression on your face. You look like he hung the moon, the stars, and all the planets to boot."

Relief that she wasn't too mad flowed, and Hunter laughed too. "Do I?"

"You do." She sighed. "I can already tell that it's not going to matter what I think."

His smile faded. "Of course it does. I can understand why you wouldn't be thrilled."

"You've never really had a boyfriend before. At least not that you ever let on."

"He's not my *boyfriend*. We just met." Although the idea of Nick being his boyfriend made Hunter want to grin, his heart dancing. "And no, I've never really dated anyone before. I was too…in my own way."

She laughed ruefully. "I can understand that." Taking a big breath, she blew it out. "Okay. I don't love that he's so much older than you, but you're a grown man yourself now. Even though you'll always be my little boy." She glanced toward the closed front door. "He's waiting outside? Maybe I should go say hello."

Hunter groaned. "*Mom.* Not right now, okay? We have to get to the mall."

She sighed noisily. "All right. You're off the hook for now. Are you coming home tonight?"

"Yeah." Although he ached to think of spending the night away from Nick, he did want to catch up with his mom. "I'll get takeout, and we can have a late dinner when you're home from work."

"That sounds lovely."

He smiled tentatively. "I know this is unexpected. For all of us! It's just been…" A little bubble of joy escaped him with a laugh. "It's been amazing."

She smiled back. "I distantly remember that feeling. Infatuation can be a glorious thing. And you're an intelligent young man. I trust your judgment, and that you'll always stay safe."

"*Yes*," he muttered, rolling his eyes.

Laughing, she kissed his cheek. "I'm still your mother. Always going to nag."

"I know." He kissed her back, then pulled her into a hug. "Thanks for being so cool, Mom. I'm really, really lucky."

She squeezed him tight. "I love you, sweetie. If Nick Spini hurts you, I know how to make it look like an accident."

He laughed and pulled back. "Let's hope it doesn't come to that. Oh! You're working the night on Christmas Eve, right? And Heather and Rick are coming Boxing Day?"

"Yep. They're spending Christmas with Rick's parents."

"John and Desmond invited us for dinner on Christmas Day. I figure since you'll be sleeping until the afternoon, it's kind of perfect." John had apparently guessed there was something going on between Hunter and Nick, and he was delighted by it, much to Hunter's relief.

"Well, that would be lovely." She gave him a knowing look. "And will Nick also be in attendance?"

"Yeah." Hunter tried not to smile, but that giddy joy bubbled through him again.

"I look forward to it. And not only so I can grill him." She winked.

"Thanks, Mom. You really are being awesome about this."

"Well, you're an adult." She inhaled deeply and blew it out. "I'd ideally like to lock you in your room and chase away Nick Spini with a shotgun, but since that's not an option, I'm going to be chill. Ish. Now you'd better get going. The kids are waiting for Santa and his elf."

BY SUNDAY NIGHT, Hunter was so ready to never, ever wear the damn candy-cane tights again. It seemed like everyone in Pinevale had come to the mall to see the sexy Santa, but the last stragglers had finally gone.

And now he and Nick could…what?

Hopefully pick up where they'd left off, but was Hunter getting ahead of himself? After spending the night alone, he'd missed Nick more than he'd thought possible, but the day had been so busy. John had been in the storeroom when Hunter had arrived that morning, so there had been no privacy. Hunter and Nick hadn't so much as brushed hands all day, let alone kissed or anything.

He itched to throw himself in Nick's arms once they reached the freezing storeroom, the cold air a relief after the sweltering heat of the mall. Yet he held back, watching Nick stretch his spine, his hands on his lower back and fake belly sticking out.

"Thank Christ that's over," Nick muttered.

"Yeah." *But what about us?* Nick hadn't said anything to make Hunter think he wanted to call it off—whatever *it* was—but Hunter's mind had spun all day, taking a little thread of doubt and whirling it into a massive ball of uncertainty that now lodged in his chest.

As Nick struggled to unhook the white beard, Hunter hurried over, his heart pounding. "Here." He went up on his tiptoes, déjà vu washing over him as Nick's big hands came around his waist to steady him.

As Hunter unhooked the beard and freed him from it, Nick murmured, "Thanks."

Still holding the beard, Hunter didn't move away, gazing up at Nick, who watched him with a little frown. Was he being crazy? He should just kiss him and—

John bustled into the storeroom, and Hunter tripped away from Nick, his heart thumping rapidly. "Hi!" he practically yelled.

John burst out laughing. "Don't worry, kid. I can handle a little PDA. He grinned. "I knew sparks were flying from the first day you two met. And don't give me that look, Nick. Let me enjoy being right."

Hunter tried to laugh. "I'm just not used to…" Fidgety and self-conscious, he stared at the bells on his shoes.

"It's all right." Nick smoothed a hand over Hunter's back and gently squeezed the back of his neck.

Hunter exhaled, the tension easing. "Okay."

He wouldn't do that if he didn't like me anymore. Right?

"This is really nice to see." John beamed at them. "Really nice. You two make a great couple."

"All right, all right," Nick groused, but he was almost smiling as he unbuttoned his Santa jacket to pull out the padding.

Hunter's heart leapt. *A couple.* Was that what they were? It was still too soon to really say, right? God, he had missed Nick desperately the night before. It was ridiculous since he'd slept alone his whole life, but his bed had seemed so cold and empty.

When he'd spent the nights at the farm, Nick's big body had curled around him, warm and comforting. Even when they'd shifted during sleep, Nick had always seemed to end up with an arm over Hunter's waist or nuzzling him close.

Had Nick missed him as much? The worry returned full force, despite Hunter's best efforts to chill the eff out. Maybe Nick had been relieved to sleep alone again. He'd told Hunter not to masturbate last night, implying that they'd be together again Sunday night. Hunter had totally disobeyed, the urge to think of Nick and get off simply too strong. But perhaps he'd also assumed too much?

Maybe Nick had had his fill, and now that they were finished with their duties at Santa's Village, this would be it. Maybe—

"What's wrong?" Nick asked, brow creased as he reached out to take hold of Hunter's shoulder.

"Nothing!" Hunter answered too quickly.

Nick's frown deepened, but he let go, and they both turned as John swore under his breath. Nick asked him, "Everything okay?"

John sighed. "I was hoping we'd be able to use the basement over at St. Mary's on Tuesday afternoon, but they're booked with childcare since the kids are out of school. We had plans for Toys and Turkeys to do a charity lunch: buy a hot dog and give a family a turkey this Christmas, but the original venue fell through.

We've had all the food and soft drinks donated, but we need a big enough space. Thursday's Christmas Eve, so we planned a big final push for fundraising Tuesday to buy out what's left in the stores and get everything delivered. It'll be good for the local businesses too."

"The mall's already half empty," Nick said. "Why not here?"

John scowled. "Red tape with the property management office. I'd have to get a permit. There's no time for that."

The perfect solution popped into Hunter's mind, and he shoved away his worry about his relationship with Nick to focus on it. "Could you do it outside? You know, a winter wonderland thing? Hot chocolate and snowman-making contests. Crafts for the kids?" He glanced at Nick. "Maybe do a raffle, and the winner gets to cut down their own tree?"

Nick jolted at that, narrowing his gaze on Hunter. "No. Forget it."

"Why not? You have the space and the most winter-wonderland location possible. I know most people will already have their trees, but some leave it until the last minute, so the raffle could be a big hit. And I bet people would come from all over for a one-day-only holiday charity extravaganza on a Christmas tree farm."

"Yes," Nick agreed sourly. "The key word

there being *people*." He looked to John, who grinned. "*No.*"

Hunter sighed dramatically, raising and then dropping his shoulders. "I guess the needy kids won't get toys or turkey on Christmas. Sucks to be them."

"Oh, for fuck's sake," Nick grumbled.

Trying not to grin, Hunter promised, "It'll be awesome. I'll plan it, and you don't have to do anything." And he would have an excuse to go back to the farm, one way or the other.

"Woo-hoo!" John high-fived Hunter. "Strong work, kid. This Grinch doesn't stand a chance with you around." He tapped his phone. "Okay, I've got to run now, but let's talk tomorrow and brainstorm activities." He winked at Nick. "Like he said, Hunter and I will work it all out, and you won't have to worry your pretty head about it."

Nick pressed his lips together. "I suggest you leave before I change my mind."

John backed away, his hands in the air. "I'm already gone. Security will be here in a few hours to make the rounds, but for now you're the only people left. When you go, make sure this door locks behind you, okay?" He pressed the metal bar on the storeroom door to the back parking lot, a gust of arctic air blowing in. "Toodles!"

"How did I just get talked into that?" Nick muttered.

Hunter almost said something cheeky about how Nick couldn't resist him, but doubt bit his tongue. What if Nick really was pissed? And *was* Hunter going back with him to the farm? Had he overstepped?

"What's wrong? You got your way—you should be thrilled." Having stripped down to his white undershirt, still wearing the Santa pants and boots, Nick looked just as he had when Hunter had first seen him.

Ignoring the bolt of lust, Hunter removed his green hat, his sweaty hair probably sticking up all over. He toyed with the hat's fuzzy white pom-pom. "Just wondering…. Am I coming back with you to the farm tonight? I mean, most of the work is done, right? So I wasn't sure if you wanted…"

There was only silence, and Hunter had to look up, his heart in his throat. Nick stared at him, his hands held up to his sides, puzzlement plain in his expression. Shaking his head, he said, "I thought we talked about it? You said you should spend a night at home, and then I assumed you'd be coming back." Something flickered across his face, his brow furrowing. "But if you don't want to…"

"I want to!" Hunter exclaimed too eagerly.

He huffed out an embarrassed laugh. "I'm not very good at playing it cool, as you can tell. I really want to come back. You just never said it explicitly?"

A small smile tugged on Nick's lips. "So then you started getting in your own way."

Hunter had to laugh. "Exactly."

Nick closed the few feet between them, taking Hunter's face in his rough hands and kissing him soundly. Exhaling as they parted, Hunter looped his arms around Nick's broad back, grinning.

He likes me. He still likes me.

Nick said, "Since we're having Christmas dinner at John and Desmond's with your mother, I assumed it was clear that we're… Well, that we're continuing." He reached up to smooth a hand over Hunter's damp hair. "At least, I'd really like to continue. See where this goes." He grimaced. "I know you're going back to the city in January, but until then…"

"Uh-huh?" Hunter leaned into his touch. The thought of going back to Toronto filled him with dread, and he focused on Nick. The future could wait.

"Until then, I want to be with you as much as possible. Is that *explicit* enough?" Then he whispered in Hunter's ear with a warm puff, "I'll be more explicit from now on. *Very* explicit."

Shuddering, Hunter pressed against him. "That sounds good. Really good. So…" He peered up at Nick. "This is a thing? Between us? You're not sick of me or anything?"

Nick regarded him seriously. "Not at all. I missed you last night." He laughed softly, like he was surprised by it. "House felt too quiet. Poor Ella is bereft."

"Awww." His heart swelled. "I can't wait to see her. And I missed you too. I couldn't get to sleep missing you, so I had to—" He broke off, biting his lip.

Nick's dark eyebrows rose. "You had to what? Were you a bad boy, Hunter?"

Swallowing hard, he nodded. "I missed you so much. I couldn't resist."

"Mmm. But I told you not to touch yourself. How naughty of you." He ran a hand over Hunter's ass, not squeezing or slapping, but with…intent.

Desire firing through him, Hunter whispered, "I'm sorry, Daddy. Let's go home, and you can punish me."

Nick blinked, opening his mouth, then closing it. Hunter realized what he'd said—*home*—and was about to clarify when Nick swooped down and kissed him, taking his breath away with the commanding sweep of his tongue as he lifted Hunter clear off his feet.

Putting him down, both of them breathing hard, Nick muttered, "Yes. Let's go." Then he swore. "I forgot my thermos out there."

"I'll go with you." Hunter needed to touch, and he threaded their fingers together as they re-entered the deserted, sweltering mall. He realized it was the first time they'd held hands, and he grinned to himself, loving how big and rough Nick's hand was, and how secure his grasp.

The bells on Hunter's elf shoes dinged merrily, echoing as they hurried over the cobblestone brick. The lights were low in the stores that were left, but the strings of Christmas lights still shone around Santa's Village.

Nick bent by the bench, grabbing the thermos he'd tucked under it. The Santa pants hugged his ass. Standing on the curving candy path, Hunter's throat went dry. Fuck, Nick was so *gorgeous*, and Hunter's dick swelled at the promise of getting to be naked with him again soon. He pressed the heel of his hand against his junk, failing to bite back a little groan.

Turning to him, Nick's eyes went dark. *Predatory.* Hunter whipped his hand back, his breath catching. He waited, watching as Nick seemed to consider. Nick's dark hair was mussed after wearing the Santa hat all day, and the colored fairy lights caught the glints of silver on his head and in his beard. His dark chest hair shadowed the white tank top.

Then Nick's hands moved to the thick belt holding up the red velvet pants. He unbuckled it, and Hunter's pulse zoomed. Nick unzipped the pants and sat on the bench at the heart of Santa's Village, spreading his legs. His black briefs were visible in the V of his open pants, but he didn't expose himself fully.

"Come here," he commanded.

Glancing around the narrow strip of the deserted old mall, a thrill sang in Hunter's veins. John had mentioned the security cameras were broken, at least. "But someone might…"

"Come. Here." Nick raised an eyebrow. "Good elves obey Santa."

Hunter giggled nervously, his cock swelling thicker in his tights as he approached, his shoes ringing. He stopped in front of Nick and breathlessly asked, "Do I get to sit on Santa's lap?"

Nick wordlessly patted his left thigh, and Hunter perched on it, clasping his hands together. His too-short green elf jacket rode up, totally exposing the bulge in his tights.

Nick asked, "Have you been naughty or nice?"

"Um, naughty." He practically shook with

anticipation, blood rushing south.

"Hmm." Nick spread his hand over Hunter's lower back, heavy and firm, his gaze focused on Hunter's with laser precision. "What did you do?"

"I jerked off last night. Thinking of you."

"Even though I told you not to?"

"Yes," Hunter breathed, excitement and nerves battling.

"Show me."

Hunter jolted. "What?" He glanced around. "You mean…*here*? Now? I can't!"

"Are you going to be a bad boy and disobey your daddy again?" Nick gripped Hunter's ass. "I'll have to spank you."

"That's not really incentive to be good," he blurted.

Nick's face creased with a smile, and he laughed softly. "Fair point." He breathed deeply, and his smile faded. "But I think I need to spank you anyway."

Without any further warning, he lifted Hunter by the waist, his muscular arms flexing as he turned him over his lap. Hunter squawked, scrambling for balance, bracing his hands on the side of the bench, his stupid shoes ringing as he dug in his toes to steady himself.

He sucked in a breath as Nick spread a hand over his ass, waiting until Hunter stopped fidgeting and had himself braced. Then Nick tugged down the tights and Hunter's boxer briefs to bare his ass.

At least it was warm given the heat of the mall, but Hunter still felt goosebumps spread over his exposed skin. The tights were caught on his junk in the front, tugging on his cock.

He waited, panting already. He dug his blunt nails into the wood of the old bench, staring at the plywood floor, painted in a candy-cane swirl. Was Nick going to say anything else, or was he—

Nick's palm came down, and Hunter yelped, jerking. It wasn't super hard—just enough to make a *smack* in the silence of the mall, the sound making Hunter's dick swell even more.

"Naughty boy," Nick chided.

Anticipating the next spank, Hunter held his breath. Then squirmed impatiently, his heart thudding. He whimpered, and Nick soothed his palm over his ass.

"Shh. I've got you. You don't have to worry about anything. Do you trust me?"

Hunter exhaled the breath that had gotten knotted in his throat. "Yes, Daddy."

"Good boy."

Nick's hand slapped down again, and again, alternating cheeks, and Hunter moaned, the anxiety melting, a sweet tension remaining as his arousal intensified. He was uncomfortable sprawled the way he was, yet that added to his pleasure at being under Nick's power, spread over his lap and held down.

It was *perfect*.

The smacks on his ass had him crying out, thrusting against Nick's lap and the answering hardness Hunter felt there. "Oh God," he groaned. The mix of pain and pleasure whited out his vision, and he squeezed his eyes shut, abandoning himself to it.

"Do you want to come?" Nick asked in a growl.

"Yes!" Hunter humped Nick's thighs desperately. "Please, Daddy."

"You were so naughty. I think you have to show me what you did first."

He opened his eyes, gripping the side of the bench and twisting his neck to look up at Nick. "Huh?"

"Bad boys need to learn their lessons." With strong hands on Hunter's hips, Nick lifted and turned him so Hunter sat on both his legs now, with his back against Nick's chest.

Fully exposed if anyone did appear.

Nick slid his hand over the front of Hunter's groin where his tights and underwear snagged on his straining cock, cupping him. "Show me," he ordered.

"Someone could come in! John might come back."

"Show me how you disobeyed me." Nick's tone was steely in his ear. "Push down your tights to your ankles. Spread your legs."

Holy shit, was he really doing this? Legs shaking, Hunter lifted to pull down his underwear and the damn candy-cane tights to the tops of the black shoes, the bells tinkling. "I… I don't…" Sweat rolled down his spine under his elf coat in the too-warm air.

It seemed so wrong to be doing this in Santa's Village, with Christmas lights and merry gingerbread and candy decorations around them. The bench where kids had told Santa their wishes. So wrong—which of course made Hunter's blood run even hotter as he spread his legs as far as he could, his throbbing dick standing free.

"Show me how you touch yourself," Nick ordered, his teeth grazing Hunter's earlobe.

Gasping, Hunter wrapped his right hand around his dick, automatically swiping the drops of precum from the tip and easing down his foreskin. "Oh, fuck," he mumbled.

He was doing it—he was jacking himself in the middle of Treeview Mall, sitting on Nick's lap in Santa's Village, Nick's hard cock nudging his ass.

"Fuck, I'm going to come so hard," he cried, arching up into his hand, his dick leaking and flushed dark red.

"You're so beautiful." Nick's whisper was hot in Hunter's ear, his hands rough as he gripped Hunter's hips. "You were a bad boy, but I'm so proud of you now."

Sweat dampened Hunter's neck, and he thought he might burst from the heat—Nick at his back and under him, the hot air of the mall, and the fire blazing through his body, centering on his cock and balls, which drew tight.

"You need it, don't you, baby?"

"*Yes*," he whined. He was so close. He strained, stroking himself faster, his gasps loud.

"Show me how good boys come for their daddies," Nick ordered.

Whole body tensing, the bells ringing as he flexed his feet and leaned back against Nick, working himself frantically, Hunter's cries were high and loud. He chased the orgasm that was just beyond reach, suddenly catching it, the pleasure exploding.

Shuddering on a strangled moan, Hunter came all over his green elf coat, spraying himself as white-hot bliss gripped him. It dripped down over his hand, and he milked himself, panting and whimpering as he relaxed, boneless in Nick's strong grasp.

He was butter against Nick's chest, which heaved with deep, excited breaths, his cock like stone under Hunter's ass. Nick picked up Hunter's sticky right hand, rasping, "Taste yourself."

Moaning, he obeyed, licking the earthy, salty fluid from his skin, dipping his tongue between his fingers, his balls twitching at how deliciously *dirty* it was.

"Can I taste you too, Daddy?" he asked breathlessly.

Nick groaned, urging Hunter to his feet and turning him. Hunter's legs were jelly, and he happily dropped to his knees between Nick's thighs, his shaking hands tugging Nick free. The red velvet pants were soft under his palms as he pushed Nick's legs open wider.

When he took Nick in his mouth eagerly, he imagined what they must look like: Santa in his village, a bare—and red—assed elf between his legs, sucking his big cock. It sent fresh lust rushing through Hunter, and he hummed around the hot flesh filling his mouth.

Nick's hands tangled in Hunter's hair. "So good. *Yes.* Good boy. Harder."

Hunter hollowed his cheeks, sucking like his life depended on it, and clumsily took hold of Nick's heavy, hairy balls with his hand. It was clearly the right thing to do, because Nick jerked, his cock choking Hunter as it swelled even bigger.

He came, groaning, his fingers tight in Hunter's hair. Hunter had to pull back, gasping and swallowing, spit and semen leaking from his mouth. Their eyes locked, and Nick sprayed the last bit of his climax on Hunter's face, hitting his cheek and wet lips.

"Fuck," Nick mumbled. He lurched forward and kissed Hunter messily, licking his splattered face and feeding the jizz to him with his tongue, the mingled taste of them both filling Hunter's mouth.

They parted, breathing heavily. Hunter glanced around, smiling. "Well, I guess Santa's Village went out with a bang."

Nick's laughter rumbled in his chest, a grin brightening his face. There was a white streak in his beard, and Hunter swiped at it with his finger and sucked it clean. "Am I on the nice list now, Santa Daddy?"

Nick chuckled. "Yes. Maybe I should keep the suit?"

"Hell yes."

"You realize you're keeping yours too. Santa needs his elf, after all." He ran his hand tenderly over Hunter's bare ass, the skin still hot from the spanking. Hunter wished he could see how red it was. Nick added, "No one else will ever get to see you in this costume but me."

Ever.

Thrilling at Nick's words, Hunter leaned up and kissed him, sucking on Nick's tongue before pulling back to whisper against his lips, "Only you, Daddy."

Chapter Nine

"ARE YOU SURE about this?" Hunter asked. "You've already donated your time in Santa's Village."

Dawn still streaked the cloudy sky orange over the horizon of snow-capped green, but Nick and Hunter were already out on a distant acre. Nick nodded. "I'm sure." He'd agreed, and it really was for a good cause.

Hunter bit his lip, his cheeks pink in the crisp, cold morning air. The pom-pom on his woolen hat bounced as he shifted boot to boot. "But I kind of forced you into hosting this fundraiser. I mean, you couldn't really say no."

"I tried," Nick noted dryly, but he didn't really mind.

You already can't deny him anything, can you?

Nick couldn't argue with Eric's sly observation. To Hunter, he added, "I hate to think of kids without a Christmas tree. John's worked his ass off to collect presents and food for these families. They need trees to put the toys under."

Hunter beamed at him like a heart-eyes emoji come to life, and Nick *had* to smile back. Hunter said, "You're really just a big softie, you know that?"

He's right, of course. Smart lad, and you should keep him around.

Grumbling with an exaggerated scowl, Nick fired up the chainsaw, cutting off the light, cheery sound of Hunter's laughter. He felled a Scotch pine that could have grown another year but was plenty big enough to fill a living room corner.

There was a ton to do before the fundraising event for Toys and Turkeys that afternoon, so they'd woken early. Nick had wanted to stay snuggled under the covers with Hunter warm and sweet in his arms, kissing Nick's chest and neck, his hair sticking up adorably. But he had to plow a makeshift parking lot in the small field to the east of the head of his driveway after they dealt with the trees.

Hunter heaved up the tree and put it through the baler, and they fell into a rhythm that was already shockingly familiar. Hunter had taken to the work like a fish to water, and pride flowed through Nick as he watched Hunter stacking a few baled trees.

Hunter glanced up when he was done. "What?" He smiled uncertainly. He breathed a little heavily, puffs of air clouding in the cold.

"Nothing." Nick turned to the next grid, sawing through the trunk of another pine.

The thing was, after the holidays this would all be over. Nick would be back out on the land on his own. Ella barked in the distance, as if to remind him he wouldn't be completely alone. He just hoped she hadn't discovered a skunk den.

He sighed to himself as he sawed another tree. After so many years of solitude, it was ridiculous that he didn't want Hunter to leave. That the thought of a quiet January and February—months when he didn't work as much and caught up on reading, watching TV, and generally hibernated—filled him with dread.

You've been alone too long and you know it, my love. He fits with you. Birds of a feather, like the song goes.

Nick argued with Eric in his mind, which was insane since it wasn't actually Eric. He argued that Hunter was too young, and surely he'd want to go back to Toronto and date other men and live his life. Not be stuck in the middle of nowhere with Nick.

Eric calmly refuted the arguments, and Nick couldn't get "Sleigh Ride" out of his head, humming it under his breath and sneaking glances at Hunter.

It had snowed again, and they stood in it up to their knees aside from the space he'd plowed for the baler. The boughs of the trees were heavy with fluffy, slightly wet snow—perfect for making snowmen. It was five degrees below freezing, and the wind was calm, the perfect winter weather. Cold enough not to be slushy, but not biting and unpleasant.

Turning off the chainsaw, Nick called, "Do you want to chop down the last one?"

Hunter's face lit up. "Yeah? Okay." He brushed dead needles from his gloves and neared. He'd learned the axe well, although it was tough work since he was slight. Nick handed him the chainsaw.

"Whoa." Hunter held it uneasily. "Heavy."

"Safety's obviously the most important thing," Nick said, taking him through the ins and outs, Hunter listening carefully and nodding.

When Hunter felled the tree with the chainsaw, he whooped with joy, making sure to turn the machinery off properly and engage the safety lock. "I did it!" He put down the chainsaw on a tarp spread on the snow.

"You did." Nick grinned at him, spreading his legs and digging in when Hunter threw himself into his arms.

"Thank you." Hunter kissed him. "For everything. I never thought I'd be good at stuff like this."

"You're very good at it." Nick nipped his jaw. "This, and…other things." He'd tried to maintain a businesslike manner when they were out on the farm, but what the hell. "We'd better load up these trees and get back to the house. John and Des will be here soon to help set up."

"I hope it'll go okay." A furrow appeared between his brows. "Maybe I should have—"

"It's going to be perfect. Trust me."

Exhaling, Hunter nodded. "I do." He smiled softly, kissing Nick again, and Nick held him close, deciding they could take a few more minutes.

THERE WERE SO many people.

Nick leaned against the barn, the inside of which was off limits to visitors, a no-entry sign tacked to the sliding door. The many, many visitors had started arriving at eleven sharp, and somehow, they just kept coming as the afternoon wore on.

That's a good thing, remember?

"Yeah, yeah," Nick muttered to Eric's teasing voice. But it *was* a good thing, and though he'd needed to escape the crowd for a few minutes, he was undeniably pleased.

Hunter and John had planned an incredible event in only two days. In the open space near the barn, they'd set up a dozen folding tables and chairs lent by one of the local churches. They'd decorated the tables with garlands and hung the barn door with a massive fresh wreath strung with red ribbon. Nick had cut the big boughs for the wreath and other hanging decorations.

Des was judging the hourly snowpeople-making contest, and children laughed and shrieked, snowballs flying. Adults stood in clumps, chatting and sipping coffee, cider, or hot chocolate. The propane barbecues roasted a steady supply of hot dogs and chestnuts, and families sat at the tables eating eagerly.

John had borrowed a portable sound system to play carols, protected under a tarp from the gentle flurries that had started around noon as more clouds had moved in. The weather was meant to stay calm, though, and Nick hoped the weather report was correct this time.

What, you don't want to be snowed in with all these people? Eric teased. *Just Hunter. Can't say I blame you.*

Still, Nick had to admit it was nice seeing people so happy and festive. He'd talked to folks he hadn't seen in years, even some old friends who'd come at John's invitation. They'd ohhed and ahhed over Hunter, and Nick had found himself making dinner plans, only half-reluctantly.

The raffle to cut down your own tree had proved a big success. They'd drawn one winner earlier since people were coming and going, and would do another soon. It had actually been all right to take the winner onto the farm and show him how to use the axe to chop. Hunter had come along, beaming.

And of course Ella was in her element, ecstatic over so many new people to meet and all the attention she was getting. Nick watched her with a smile, his gaze then finding Hunter. His smile deepened, warmth filling his chest.

At a table, Hunter leaned over craft supplies—Styrofoam balls, spray paint, glitter, and macaroni—helping a little girl make a tree ornament. He was patient as the girl fumbled, and though Nick was too far away to hear what he was saying, he knew Hunter was being kind to her.

He couldn't tear his eyes away. He wanted Hunter too much. Not just in his bed, but…all the time. Which was *ludicrous* since they'd known each other barely more than a week.

We knew after the first date. Do you remember? Eric asked.

Memories wheeled through Nick's mind—the coffee date that had become lunch, and then dinner at another restaurant, then drinks, then back to Eric's house for a night of sex. They'd been inseparable after.

Perhaps this is just how it goes with you. Hunter's practically moved in already, and you don't want him to go anywhere. Do you?

Boots crunched in the snow, approaching, and Nick pushed away the thoughts and Eric's imaginary voice, tearing his gaze from Hunter, who clapped as the girl held up her macaroni creation.

Nick focused on a woman who neared the barn. She was perhaps a little older than he was, small and golden-haired, a little plump in a puffy red ski jacket, her cheeks pink under a hat with reindeer antlers. When she smiled tentatively, he knew, recognizing the shape of her mouth.

"Nick? I don't know if you remember me."

He stood up straight, pushing away from

the side of the barn. "Pam, isn't it?"

"Yes." She glanced over at Hunter. "You and my son have been getting to know each other."

"We have," Nick agreed, trying to keep his voice even. He was forty-six goddamn years old, yet he felt like a schoolboy picking up his prom date with a cheap corsage in his sweaty hands. Not that he had ever done that. He'd gone to the prom with a lesbian friend.

"He's quite taken with you," Pam said. "To be honest, I don't know how to feel about it."

"Neither do I."

She laughed. "I appreciate the honesty."

He shoved his gloved hands in the pockets of his dark coat. "I never planned on this. Or expected it. Not in the slightest."

"I believe that." She brushed a snowflake from her nose. "I haven't seen him this happy in… In a long time. He's been so anxious and unsure of what to do with his life."

"Yes. I suppose he should go back to Toronto in the new year. Give it another go."

She frowned. "I suppose. But I'm not so sure."

Despite himself, Nick's heart skipped. "No?"

"He's been so hung up on what he *should* do. Get a 'real' job in an office. Even if it makes him miserable." She looked over to where Hunter now chatted with an adult couple, gesturing animatedly toward the acres of trees that extended off into the distance. "He's really enjoyed the work here."

"He's a fast learner."

"You seem to give him confidence. That's a big point in your favor."

Nick chuckled. "Good to know."

Her smile faded. "I just don't want my son's heart to get broken. I know you suffered a great loss with Eric. He was a wonderful man."

Throat suddenly thick, Nick nodded.

"Please make sure you know what you're doing. Don't make promises you can't keep. I've been on the receiving end of that. I don't want it for Hunter. If this is only a Christmas fling, that's fine—just make sure he knows that. If you can't give him more, be upfront. That's all I ask."

Nick nodded again and cleared his throat. "Fair enough."

She smiled. "All right. I'll see you for Christmas dinner, I understand? I look forward to it."

"Me too."

As she walked away, a little tug of panic bloomed. *Did* he know what he was doing? More than just fucking Hunter, he was practically living with him already. Having Christmas dinner with his mother.

He'd told Hunter he wanted to continue on with whatever it was between them, and he did. But what *was* growing between them? It was happening so quickly. Was Nick making promises he couldn't keep?

The carols and shrieks of laughter and all the *people* were entirely too much now, and he escaped into the dark cold of the barn, closing the door firmly behind him. It smelled of pine and earth, faint light filtering in through gaps in the wood.

The last thing he wanted was to break Hunter's heart—or his own.

Chapter Ten

INHALING THE COLD night air deeply, Hunter ran after Ella behind the house toward the river, his legs straining in the drifts. She barked around the rubber chicken in her mouth as if to complain he was too slow, racing back to drop it into the unbroken snow at his feet. Laughing, he threw it again, and she bolted off in pursuit.

He was wonderfully exhausted and a little too full of leftover hot dogs. The fundraiser had been a huge success, and Hunter felt stupidly proud of himself. Of course John had done a lot of the work, but Hunter had planned the crafts and stuff for the kids, and everyone had seemed to have fun.

Well, perhaps everyone but Nick, who had been broody and quiet that evening. He'd been friendly enough to people earlier, but all the interacting had clearly worn on him. Hunter's mom said she and Nick had "had a little talk," which was so mortifying he hadn't gotten up the nerve to ask Nick how embarrassing she'd been.

Nick hadn't been *overly* grumpy during dinner, but he hadn't said much, seeming preoccupied. Hunter had shut up and let him watch the episode of the latest superhero show they'd cued up on Netflix.

Ella slid to a stop at his feet, and Hunter whirled and threw the rubber chicken again. This time, it sailed across the frozen water and landed on the ice near the far side, a wind tunnel created by the nearby tree line having driven most of the snow on the river clear. But Ella skidded to a stop, whining by the edge.

Hunter laughed and called, "Come on, go get it!"

But she wouldn't budge, so Hunter carefully tested the ice and slid onto it, his arms out for balance. The small river likely wasn't very deep, and it felt frozen solid beneath his boots. He made his way across and bent to snatch up the chicken.

"Get off the ice!"

Hunter whirled around, his heart jumping, wheeling his arms to stay on his feet. Nick's voice had boomed in the peace of the night, and it took Hunter a moment to understand why Nick was shouting, stalking closer, inexplicable fury vibrating from him.

As it hit Hunter that Ella had likely been trained not to go on the ice—and that it was for a very particular reason—he gasped and slip-slid back toward shore, which was only ten feet or so, Ella barking from the edge.

Hunter was almost there when Nick grabbed him, lifting him practically off his feet. He felt like he was soaring the rest of the way to solid ground, landing with a thud, his hat falling off. Nick's eyes were wild, his bare fists gripping the front of Hunter's jacket. He was out in just his jeans and plaid flannel shirt, no hat or coat or any winter gear.

Their breath clouded together in sharp bursts. Maybe Hunter should have been afraid with Nick towering over him, but he wasn't. Not at all. He could see the raw terror beneath Nick's fury, and he grabbed around Nick's waist, holding on tight. "I'm sorry. I didn't think."

Squeezing his eyes shut, Nick shook his head, his fingers twitching where he held onto Hunter's coat, his whole body shaking. Hunter pulled him close, trying to hug him.

"It's okay," Hunter murmured. "Everything's okay."

Nick exhaled a mighty breath that sounded close to a sob, collapsing against him. Hunter staggered under his weight but dug his heels into the snow. No way in hell he was letting go. He pulled off his glove so he could run his fingers through Nick's hair and feel him, the hot gusts of Nick's breath moist against his neck.

"I'm here," Hunter whispered. "It's okay."

But Nick shoved away from him. He swiped a hand across his face. His voice was hoarse. "No. I can't do this. I *shouldn't* do this. It's a mistake."

Now fear snaked through Hunter, ice down his spine. "What do you mean?"

Nick drew himself up, steel in his voice, like the standoffish, haughty man Hunter had first met in that storeroom. "This was a mistake, having you here. You should go."

"*What?*" He couldn't believe what he was hearing. "You don't mean that."

"I do. This never should have happened between us. Now go. And don't come back." He stomped toward the house, Ella whining and looking between them but following Nick with agitated barks.

Hunter stood motionless by the frozen river, his breath white puffs in the frigid air, his bare fingers tingling. After everything they'd shared, it was just over? He was supposed to leave with his tail between his legs because Nick said so?

Fuck. That.

With a growl, Hunter followed, his boots crunching in the snow. By the woodpile, Nick turned and stared incredulously as Hunter marched toward him. "I told you to go."

"No." Hunter stopped in front of him, squaring his shoulders. "First off, I'm not walking back to Pinevale."

Nick grimaced as if he hadn't considered that. "You can take the pickup. I'll get it another day. It doesn't matter."

"As long as I do what you say and leave you alone and never come back?"

Gaze on his unlaced boots, Nick nodded.

"That's not how this works. Not out here. You're Daddy in bed, and I'll happily do what you say. But you don't get to give me orders when we're not fucking. You don't get to decide things between us without even *talking* to me. In a snap of your fingers this is over? No. I'm not going anywhere."

"I told you, this was a mistake." Nick's jaw was clenched, but his voice shook. He still looked down.

"Why? Because you saw me on the ice and got scared something would happen to me?

Because you care about me?"

Shaking his head, Nick backed up, hitting the stack of firewood. Ella whined again, tense by Nick's side. Nick's throat worked, his breath short. The front door of the house was standing open, and Nick snapped toward it. "Ella! Inside."

Reluctantly, she went. Hunter breathed hard, trying to figure out the right thing to say. He wanted to hold Nick again and tell him everything would be okay, but not yet. Ella followed Nick's commands always, but Hunter wasn't backing down.

"That river is frozen solid, and even if it wasn't—it's only, what, waist-deep? But it probably scared you seeing me out there because of what happened to Eric." Hunter was pretty sure it was the first time he'd said that name aloud. Nick flinched, looking up at the stars now, panting softly.

Hunter took a deep breath and continued. "I'm so, so sorry about what happened to him. I can only imagine what that was like for you. But I'm not going to let you push me away because you're afraid. You wouldn't be afraid if you didn't care about me, and I care about you too. I know we just met, but I'm falling in love with you."

Hunter's words hung in the air, and Nick

lowered his head, facing him. "I can't do this again," he rasped. "I should never have… This is why I was alone. I can't love you and have something happen. I can't. Your mother said…"

Hunter cringed. "Oh God, what?" She'd always been so cool, but he was going to freak if she'd messed with Nick's head because she was overprotective.

"It wasn't bad." Nick cleared his throat, his fingers clenching and unclenching. "She doesn't want me to break your heart or make promises I can't keep. And she's right. I can't give you this." He motioned between them with rigid jabs of his hand. "*This* is too much. Already." He laughed hollowly. "I don't even know how it happened, but it's too much. Because I can't care and lose you. I can't go through that. Not again."

"We're all going to die. And I hope it's not for a very long time for either of us. But we have to live in the meantime." He had Nick cornered, which sounded stupid since Nick was twice his size, but Hunter stepped closer slowly. He reached out tentatively, taking Nick's hand and squeezing his trembling fingers. The toes of their boots touched, their white puffs of breath mingling again.

Hunter whispered, "I want you to love me.

I want us to love each other. I want to stay here and work with you."

Nick clung to his fingers. "You want to stay? Not go back to Toronto?"

"Right. If you'll have me? I never thought of myself as outdoorsy or anything like that, but I love the fresh air and my muscles burning and being out here far away from cubicles and computers and rush hour. Have you ever ridden the subway at rush hour? If there's a hell, it's being crammed into a metal box with thousands of other people twice a day. I don't want to do it. Even if that means I'm wasting my degree or whatever, I don't want to work in an office. I want to know everything about trees and planting and harvesting—all of it. This is a real job, and I want to do it. Or at least try."

Nick blew out a long breath in a stream of white. "I want that too. The twelve- and fourteen-hour days are a lot. Maybe I've been too much of a workaholic. Having full-time help…a partner, would be good."

"They say work/life balance is vital." Hunter gave him a little smile.

Nodding, Nick exhaled again, his expression serious. "I'm sorry I was rough with you. Seeing you on the ice…" He took another deep breath and exhaled. "Please don't go out there, even if it's safe." He lifted a hand and stroked

Hunter's cheek with cold fingers. "Is that unreasonable of me?"

"No. I can do that for you. It's an easy thing to do." He still held Nick's other hand, and he squeezed gently. "Can you do something for me?"

Nick stared down into his eyes, his own softening. "Anything."

Hunter smiled gratefully, joy making a tentative return. "Don't shut me out of important decisions. Like, you know, whether or not we should be together? That's pretty important. We're equals in this, right? Even if you're in charge when we have sex?"

He didn't hesitate, squeezing Hunter's hand. "Yes. Absolutely. Even if I'm an overprotective ass sometimes."

Hunter laughed softly. "I can handle that. I know you were scared. And I'm sure it won't be the last time we argue."

Nick's lips twitched in a smile. "I'm sure not. Especially if you're moving in."

His belly flip-flopped with excitement. "Is that what you want? I got snowed in, and now I'm staying?"

Smile growing, Nick said, "Yes. Maybe it'll end in disaster, but I want you to stay. I want you with me out there." He nodded in the direction of the trees before motioning to the house behind him. "And in here." He stepped close, pressing their bodies together and taking Hunter's face in both his hands. "In my bed. *Our* bed."

"I want that too," Hunter whispered. "All of it." His pulse galloped. "And I don't want either of us to have our heart broken. So let's not, okay?"

"Deal."

"Let's have a Christmas miracle instead and be happy forever." He went up on his tiptoes and kissed Nick then, trying to tell him everything he was feeling with the steady press of his lips. He wanted to work with him and live with him and love him. He inched back, looking up into Nick's moon-glow eyes. "Take me to bed, Daddy."

Hunter's feet went out from under him, and he gasped as Nick swept him into his arms and strode to the front door. Hunter's laughter bubbled out of him, echoing in the trees standing silent guard. He loved the sensation of being aloft and secure against Nick's body.

"You're not supposed to carry me over the threshold until we get married," he teased, then bit his lip. He was only joking, but would it scare off Nick?

Nick paused under the eaves. "This is the quickest way to get you naked in bed." He strode inside the open door with his own laugh and kicked it shut.

His arms around Nick's neck, Hunter giggled. "Can't argue with that logic." Ella barked, her tail wagging, and Hunter couldn't stop laughing as Nick carried him upstairs. "Ella agrees."

When they were naked together, the curtains open to the silver night, Hunter got on his hands and knees. But Nick turned him and drew him close, kissing him with a gentle, questing tongue. Nick tasted him until Hunter's head spun, then pressed him back against the mattress, his lips exploring every inch of flesh until Hunter could only beg for more.

Nick kissed his mouth again, and Hunter could taste his own sweat and desire. Nick was heavy on top of him, surrounding him, keeping him safe and cherished. Raising his knees to his chest, Hunter cried out as Nick entered and fucked him, stretching him to the breaking point, but never too far.

Epilogue

One Year Later

"HIGHER ON YOUR side!" Hunter called, and Nick raised his end of the banner, balancing on a ladder by the trunk of one of the bare maple trees at the entrance of the farm's long driveway. John was on another ladder by a tree on the other side. Snow piled up around the ladders, the sun peeking out of the scattered clouds and making the fresh snow glitter like diamonds.

In his parka, woolen hat, and work boots, Hunter stood in the middle of the curving country road as he peered up. Nick couldn't hear any vehicles approaching, but still. "Would you hurry up and get off the road?"

Hunter huffed a laugh and stepped closer. "Okay. It's good."

Nick and John climbed down, and the three of them stood back enough to peer up at the banner.

"This is going to be epic," John said. "I can't believe Hunter talked you into it again. But I also can't believe he convinced you to let people cut down their own trees this season."

Nick grumbled. "Me either."

Hunter grinned. "It wasn't so bad, and you know it."

"Maybe not." Nick tried to scowl but didn't succeed, and Hunter's grin brightened.

Along with working with Nick out on the farm, Hunter had taken on the marketing and communications for the business. He had ideas to grow revenue. One was to open the farm to the public for three weekends as the holiday season began at the end of November, letting people cut down their own trees and offering sleigh rides, hot chocolate and snacks, and wreath-making.

"Actually, the weekends were a huge success," Hunter added. To John, he said, "And he knows it."

"Oh, you've got this Grinch's number all right." John winked at Nick merrily, pushing his wire-frame glasses up his nose. "Before you know it, you'll be playing Santa again, Nick."

"Never going to happen." Nick glared. "*Never.*"

"But you were so good at it!" John insisted, laughing and raising his hands. "Don't worry, that rundown Santa's Village is no more." He checked his watch. "Okay, I've gotta run. Des, Pam, and I will be back tomorrow morning to help set up. Oh, and Tim and his new boyfriend volunteered to come early."

"My friend Shelby's in town, so she's coming to help too," Hunter said.

John exclaimed, "It's going to be even better than last year. I can feel it!"

"Yeah, yeah," Nick muttered, but he gave his friend a smile.

"Want me to drop you guys off back up at the house?"

Hunter and Nick shared a glance, and Hunter said, "I wouldn't mind the walk, actually." Nick nodded, and they waved goodbye to John as he climbed into his SUV and drove off.

In tandem, Nick and Hunter reached for each other, clasping their gloved hands as they ambled up the long, plowed driveway, curving through the trees for a couple of kilometers. Their boots crunched in the packed snow, breath pluming in the cold air.

"I haven't walked along here since that first time," Hunter said with a smile. "Hard to believe it's been a year."

Nick squeezed his fingers. "Time flies. This journey should be a little more pleasant."

"Let's hope so." Hunter grinned, his blue eyes sparkling as he gave Nick a quick kiss with cold lips.

Playing outside, Ella greeted them like conquering heroes when she spotted them approaching the house, and they indulged her in scratches and pets until they all went inside.

Hunter chided Ella when she tried to jump up and swipe at the end of a sparkly red, gold, and green garland that had come unstuck from around one of the wooden support beams in the kitchen.

Chuckling, Nick got out the tape and fixed the garland before flipping the light switch that powered the multicolored Christmas lights strung around the bannister and along the railing of the landing along the open second-floor hallway.

The switch also powered the Christmas tree dominating the corner to the right of the fireplace. As the colored lights gleamed, silver tinsel sparkled, a hodgepodge of old and new ornaments glittering. Wrapped presents to each other filled the space below the Scotch pine. They'd learned the hard way the previous week not to put anything under there if they didn't know what it was after an incident with Ella and a box of After Eights from a vendor.

It had been forever since Nick had actually had his own Christmas tree. Ironic given he farmed the things, and he found he loved the fresh scent that filled their home.

Home.

It really was a home again. It hadn't always been easy—he and Hunter definitely argued sometimes, although the makeup sex was...*remarkable.* As was all the sex, and he was looking forward to having a lot of it in the weeks to come.

With the hard work of the year done as Christmas approached in a few short days, it was a relief. Once the charity event was over, Nick looked forward to relaxing in front of the fire with Hunter and Ella. Although he and Hunter—ninety-five percent Hunter—had somehow volunteered to host Christmas dinner, so there would be lots of cooking to do.

Lighting the stack of wood and kindling waiting, Nick smiled to himself. He'd cooked a lot more in the past year since Hunter was such an enthusiastic eater, so he didn't really mind. In fact, he relished it. Hunter liked cooking as well, and they often chopped and stirred together, listening to a podcast or audiobook, Ella at their feet hoping for them to drop something delicious.

Nick ran his fingers over the soft cotton of the three stockings hung from the wooden mantel, their names inscribed in curly gold script on the red material.

Nick, Hunter, Ella

There was an addition to the collection of framed photos as well—a selfie of him and Hunter, sweaty with their shears over their shoulders after a long day of summer work, satisfied smiles on their faces and wide-brimmed hats on their heads.

In the other corner of the living room, Hunter was humming to himself and fiddling with the old stereo. Then jazzy Christmas music flowed through the room, and Nick's heart clenched.

"Is that the Ella Fitzgerald CD?" he asked.

Hunter picked up the case. "Yep. *Ella Wishes You a Swinging Christmas.* There's a lot of her, actually." He laughed. "Oh! I just realized where our Ella got her name!"

Nick smiled softly. "Yes." He paused, then added, "Eric loved Ella Fitzgerald. I haven't listened to those old CDs in years."

Hunter's beautiful face creased. "Do you want me to turn it off?"

You'd better not. This is the greatest holiday album of all time. It deserves to be heard.

Nick smiled at Eric's voice in his head. He heard it less frequently these days, but once in a while Eric would appear with a piece of wisdom. To Hunter, Nick said, "No. It deserves to be heard. Thank you for finding it."

He turned back to tend to the fire as the wonderful smell of burning wood filled the house along with Ella's smooth, jazzy Christmas tunes. Hunter went upstairs, and Nick was humming when he heard him return, the steps creaking.

"I found something else," Hunter announced.

Nick turned, his breath stolen and desire sparking like the kindling in the fireplace. Hunter stood on the bottom step wearing the old elf costume. After a year of manual labor, the green jacket was an even smaller fit, and he'd left it open over his bare chest. The candy-cane tights were obscene, hiding nothing. His feet were bare, and the green velvet elf hat and fake ears sat on his head.

Hunter held up a bundle of white-trimmed red velvet. "Santa, I've been a very naughty boy."

"Oh, I *know* you have." Nick crooked his finger, love and lust filling him completely, making him whole.

Their Ella barked in the kitchen, Ella Fitzgerald crooning about birds of a feather as Hunter and Nick met by the hearth with hands and mouths, hearts soaring.

THE END

About the Author

Keira aims for the perfect mix of character, plot, and heat in her M/M romances. She writes everything from swashbuckling pirates to heartwarming holiday escapism. Her fave tropes are enemies to lovers, age gaps, forced proximity, and passionate virgins. Although she loves delicious angst along the way, Keira guarantees happy endings!

Discover more at:
KeiraAndrews.com